OWATONNA NOVELLAS

INCLUDING CHRISTMAS LIGHTS & VALENTINE'S HEARTS

RJ SCOTT

V.L. LOCEY

Love Lane Books

COPYRIGHT

DEDICATION

To my family who accepts me and all my foibles and quirks.
Even the plastic banana in my holster.
V.L. Locey

To every Owatonna fan who asked us to show them what
happened next for Jacob & Ryker...
And always for my family.
RJ Scott

Christmas LIGHTS

an OWATONNA Holiday Novella

RJ SCOTT & V.L. LOCEY

Love Lane Books

1

RYKER

Coach Carmichael paced the full length of the locker room, his gaze landing on each of us before he stopped right in front of Alex. This was what he did before every game. He zeroed in on one of the guys and imparted words of wisdom. Sometimes it was just a quick "get this done" with a lift of an eyebrow; other times it was this whole speech about teamwork and how good the picked-on player could be if only he did X, Y, or Z. On most occasions, he lightened the tone. Sometimes he even made a joke, although none of us laughed in case he was being ironic; none of us wanted to get on Coach's bad side after all.

Before the last game, it had been me under the spotlight, being reminded that scrappiness in the corners was a prerequisite and not a choice. I'd held his gaze, even as Alex had snickered next to me, and Jens had scrubbed his face with his hands, trying not to laugh. One turnover against Boston and I would be labeled as the guy who got sloppy in the corners for the rest of the damn season, but what everyone had failed to mention was that I'd had Brady Rowe all the fuck over me and I'd been intimidated. Every rookie had their first time breaking under intimidation, and that had been my moment, and I'd sure as hell wanted to own it. But that was the last game. This game it was Alex who would get the pep talk. I waited with bated breath and a barely held snicker at this payback.

Coach crossed his arms over his chest. "The Railers *will* put Tennant Rowe's line out against the JAR line."

I exchanged glances with Jens, who was the J in the Jens/Alex/Ryker line, or JAR as we were now known by pundits, haters, and fans alike, and he gave me a look that spoke volumes. Going up against the Railers was something that only happened a few times a year. After all, the Pennsylvania team was in the Eastern Conference, and we were in the West, but given they were third in the overall table to our scratchy twenty-third, we all knew that tonight was going to be one long-ass fight to come away with any points at all.

That's defeatist, my dad's words flew into my thoughts. He always told me that the game was won in a man's head way before he started to play, and I respected the hell out of my dad, who was coach to the same damn Railers team we were facing tonight.

"You know you'll have their best D-Men out against you, Ulfsson and Sato-West, so for fuck's sake keep your heads up and stay on task." He waved to include me and Jens. "To quote the Great One, 'skate to where the puck is going to be, not where it has been', okay? Watch for any space and play the game. I want shots on goal because tonight we're playing the statistics game."

My brain went immediately to another well-timed Gretsky quote, 'you miss a hundred percent of the shots you don't take'.

Yay for that to pop into my thoughts when we were potentially going to come away losing ten-one to one of the best teams ever fielded in the NHL.

"Coach," Alex murmured, and we all said the same. The pep talk wasn't just for Alex. It was for all of us, really, and we knew that.

"We *can* do this," Coach added and slowly turned a full three-sixty. "We *can* win against this team. We have the pieces in place. We just need to move in the right direction. Let's call the starting lineup," he instructed and handed the clipboard to Colorado, who was our backup goalie tonight, nursing a sprained groin muscle. Whether or not it was from hockey or one of his particularly active sex marathons he talked so much about , we didn't know. Still, he was there if we needed him, but on the other hand, we really hoped we didn't because just recently he'd become even more erratic than he'd been before. Colorado grinned wolfishly, then tapped the board in an imitation drum roll.

"Forwards: Jens, Cherry, Madsen; D-men: Novikov, Myers, and Lemon is our starting goalie." At that point, he fist-bumped Andre LeMans, who just sighed at the fact that his nickname had somehow become Lemon, just as Alex Garcia had become Cherry. Part of me wished I'd get a cool nickname as well, but Mads was already taken by my dad, and even though other players used it, I kind of wanted my own. One day.

Each name was met by a small cheer, and by the time we were lined up in the tunnel, waiting for warm-ups, I was pumped. This was going to be good. I just had to forget it was the Railers and focus on the fact that I'd practiced against Ten, my unofficial/official stepdad, for so long over the summer I'd begun to learn some of the things he did so well. Of course, seeing him tonight wasn't going to be fun like we'd had in the heat of summer. This was serious shit. The Raptors needed the points desperately, and I couldn't even look at my dad on the Railers bench in case he smiled at me with encouragement or was in coach mode and scowled at me as an opposing player. Unfortunately, Ten hadn't gotten the memo about avoiding me as he was waiting at the center line as I passed.

"Ry." He nodded and skated slowly away, giving me a smile that was half love and half we're-gonna-crush-you. I smiled back and returned his nod, sending a puck across the ice to land on his stick. He passed it back, and that was all we did by way of acknowledging each other as opponents.

Then after a short break, it was game on, and the Railers were three goals up in the first period with Ten's line out every single damn time the JAR line was out. There wasn't a hope in hell of them making a mistake so we could steal the puck.

But then, early in the second period, Adler Lockhart, made a mistake. He turned over the puck, and I could hear the collective gasps in the arena and probably from every single person watching this game on TV. The Railers didn't do turnovers, and at first, our line froze, and then it became obvious what had happened. Lockhart's stick had tangled after a heroic dive from our best D-Man and captain, Vlad.

Vlad shuttled the puck to Alex, and what Alex did next was a thing of beauty. He hared up the rink toward Stan Lyamin, making it look as if he was going straight to shoot, and then in a highlight reel move, he passed left to Jens, who sent it streaking from his stick onto mine. There was no way I could dust this pass off; we didn't have time. We'd caught the Railers off guard, and I had to shoot now. Otherwise, Stan would close that tiny gap he'd left, thinking Alex was firing a slap shot from the other end. Everything slowed down, instinct kicked in, and I visualized where it was going. I could feel every muscle in me screaming to make this the right shot for this moment.

When the puck left my stick, it didn't even wobble or waver. It headed straight for the hole between Stan's glove and his beloved pipes—a hole that was closing, even as the puck flew. He missed the flying rubber disc by an inch, the net straining as the puck hit it, and *somehow* the Raptors had scored against the Railers, and we had pulled a goal back. The siren sounded in the arena, the Raptors fans going wild, and I went to one knee, celebrating in the most dramatic way I could. That goal, the first I'd ever scored against my dad and Ten, was one I would remember forever.

After that, it was almost okay that we lost by four goals.

. . .

ALEX AND I MET DAD AND TEN AFTER THE GAME. WITH only three days to go until Christmas, it was hard to find any suitable place we could meet up, so we'd asked them back to our place, which had a tiny tree in one corner and lights around the arch into the kitchen. We were done with official games before Christmas, with five days off because of the way the game schedule fell for us. Not so much for the Railers, who had games in Dallas and Florida close to Christmas Day.

After tomorrow's practice and postgame analysis, my Christmas break started, although losing to the Railers five to one wasn't a brilliant result for us to discuss as a team. Whatever. *Nothing* was going to mess with my excitement at spending an entire five days with Jacob.

Ten waltzed into our place, looking all kinds of badass, then hugged me so tight I couldn't breathe.

"So proud of you, Ry," he wouldn't let me go until Dad pried him away.

"Nice goal, son," Dad said gruffly and held me almost as tight. "So fucking tight."

"What about my feint and pass?" Alex teased when we all separated, and he got included in hugs as well, along with congratulations from Ten. Alex was spending time with his family, and that included his partner, Sebastian, and I know he was apprehensive, although things had been better recently. At least Sebastian had been invited to spend time with Alex's family, so that was a win.

"Presents!" Ten announced, and I heard Dad groan. Ten had this way of going into a shop and buying *everything*. No joke. From a bargain-bin bobblehead to expensive skates, he just wanted to give everything to everyone, donating a shit ton of money to local charities anonymously and helping to make peoples' Christmases good ones.

Even Alex was in on the gift exchange, and we spent a good hour laughing and drinking beer and celebrating Christmas early. Part of me was sad that I wasn't seeing Mom and Dad in the break, but Dad was down south, and he had Ten, and as for Mom, she was on vacation in Mexico with her husband and my little sisters. Everything had worked out so well for both of them, but I knew if I'd been alone, then either Mom or Dad would have been there for me.

Only this year, I wasn't going to be alone at all.

I was going to Jacob's farm, staying in some old cabin he and his dad had spent the fall renovating. Scott was coming with Hayne, and Benoit was visiting with Ethan for at least three days. The six of us had been planning this Christmas break since the NHL bigwigs had released the schedule, and it would be so good to catch up with Scott and Ben, if only to shoot the shit and remember life before everything had gone to hell. Owatonna College seemed so long ago, and chilling with friends was exactly what I needed. Not that it was only a college reunion. After all, we'd invited Henry as well, but he was only coming out of the therapy facility for a few days and spending the time with his family this Christmas, although he didn't seem all that happy with that particular state of affairs. He was getting more morose and confused with every visit, so much so that his key therapist had suggested we stop visiting for a while.

Alex went to bed a little after two a.m., Ten pleaded exhaustion, and then it was just Dad and I, sitting by the tree in silence, enjoying each other's company, and sipping coffee, which I knew would likely keep me up.

"Is it okay if I ask you something, Dad?"

He glanced up from his coffee and smiled at me. "Always," he murmured. We'd had our bad times, Dad and I, but there was no man I wanted more in my corner in my public and private life. The question I had was very relevant to the thoughts spinning in my head right now. Jacob and I. The future.

"Did you know Ten would say yes when you asked him to marry you?"

His eyes widened a little, and then he nodded. "You have to remember Ten wasn't in a good place back then, with his injury and with the residual…" He tapped his head, and I couldn't help but recall the awfulness of that Christmas. Through it all, Dad and Ten had fought the effects of the injury to stay together and in love, and then the wedding, it had been so beautiful.

"But you knew he'd say yes, right?"

He paused, but that was my dad; the focused, calm one, he never let words fly that weren't considered and thoughtful.

"Ten is the other half of me, and despite everything, in my heart, I knew he'd say yes. Why?"

"No reason, just been thinking about things, is all."

"Is something worrying you? Is someone on the team messing with you about me and Ten?" Abruptly, he was fiercely defensive of his son, and I loved him for that.

"No way would Coach Carmichael let any of that fly," I reassured him. "I just…" I couldn't finish the sentence. The enormity of what I felt for Jacob was difficult to put into mere words.

"What is it, Ry? Are you okay?" He looked so concerned, and it didn't take much for me to see that I was coming over as a weird-ass kid who was worrying his dad.

I wanted to tell him that Jacob and I would be together forever. But he might've thought I was stupid, and say that we couldn't know what we wanted yet. Dad loved me whatever I did, but what if he said I was too young to think about tying myself to one person?

I'm twenty-four, and Jacob is my forever, I defended myself in the imaginary scenario in which Dad might think less of me or question my decisions. Of course he could be good with everything, but on the off chance he wasn't, I kept my truth that Jacob was my everything to myself for now.

"I'm fine, Dad, just happy to see you and Ten so good together."

Dad pulled me into a sideways hug.

"Love you," he said.

"I love you too."

"Merry Christmas, son."

2

JACOB

You know you're a farmer when...

There are a lot of punch lines for that old joke.

Going to bed at nine p.m. is too late on a typical day.

Your dog rides shotgun in the truck.

The great outdoors is your bathroom.

You don't enjoy eating something that you haven't grown.

Christmas means getting the same two gifts every year: a new pocketknife to replace the one you left lying on the tractor after cutting the strings off a hay bale, and new Carhartt overalls.

You check the weather as soon as you get out of bed by opening the curtains and not checking an app because your Internet only works when you're out in the hay barn, standing in the loft while balancing on one foot.

Yawning widely, I padded to my bedroom window, offered up a silent prayer, and threw the dark blue curtains open.

"Fuck." I sighed, looking down on a new foot of snow that had fallen. That would set things back at least an hour. I glanced at the clock. Ten minutes after four. Time to get the day rolling if I had any hope of meeting Ryker at our little airport at noon. He'd had to catch a kicker flight from St. Paul International to finish the final leg of his journey. My stomach flipped and flopped like a perch on a taut line, thinking of seeing him again. It had been nearly two months since we'd last held each other. I'd never really believed you could literally ache from missing a person, but I did, every hour of every day, my heart languished for Ryker.

"Right, enough!" I closed the drapes, pulled on my long johns, a pair of old jeans, a sweatshirt, a flannel shirt, and some thick hunting socks. I snuck out of my room, careful not to step on the old creaking floorboards that led me past my parents' room. Dad would still be asleep. The cold weather settling in over Minnesota was playing havoc with his bad hip. He should have had it replaced, but we didn't have any health insurance. The money to pay for that had been gobbled up by the tariffs some moron had slapped on other countries. Farmers were hurting big-time, and our family farm was teetering on the verge of bankruptcy. I paused outside their door, stopping to listen to my father's robust snores. He'd be down by six, sleeping in as it were, but I'd have the tractor warmed up and the milkers into the parlor by the time he limped down to the milking parlor. Or I would if I stopped dawdling in the hallway.

Ten minutes later, I was outside shoveling snow, clearing a path for Dad so he wouldn't have to exert his bad hip. It was backbreaking work, but soon enough I was in the barn and had the old Massey-Ferguson we'd bought at an auction—another local farm being sold—plugged in. Then it was back to the house to make coffee and fill the two thermoses my dad and I took to the barn. As the coffee perked, I cracked eggs into Mom's favorite cast-iron frying pan and stirred up a mound of scrambled eggs. Toast followed and some sausages from the pig we'd raised last summer. We'd never done too many pigs, but the piglet had been a runt, and so we'd gotten him for free. Turned out that runt porked up to over four hundred pounds when he'd been weighed at the butchers.

"Honey, you don't have to cook too," Mom said as she shuffled into the kitchen, hair brushed and her winter work clothes on. She'd taken to helping out as well, since Dad could barely walk anymore. "You do enough around here."

I pecked her cheek as she wiggled in beside me to give the sausages a poke with a fork. Juices flowed out of the fat links and made a sizzling smoke that filled the kitchen. My stomach rumbled. Mom patted my belly, then set the table, chatting about Ryker and the old cabin we'd renovated. Renovated was kind of a stretch. More like Dad and I had covered the windows in plastic, chased out the coons that had been living there, filled the holes in the walls where the porcupines had chewed through, allowing the coons to move in, and cleaned the fireplace.

"Why don't you let me handle setting up the calf pens today?" I glanced back at her. She looked tired. Waking up tired seemed wrong.

"No, I'm fine."

"I can get them set up before I go pick up Ryker," I told her. She frowned, knowing that arguing with me was like arguing with my father. As much as he and I butted heads, we were cut from that same stubborn, proud Minnesota farmer cloth. "The first calves aren't due to hit the ground until mid-January."

"Damn Curtis Young and his stupid shitty fences," Mom muttered under her breath. I nodded silently. Yeah, it sucked that our neighbor's bull had walked through a hole in his shitty fencing last spring, bulled through our electric fence, and fucked just about every cow we had out in the pasture that day. We much preferred having our calves born a little later, say mid-February through March, but good old Festus the Hereford clearly had other plans for our dairy cows. "Jacob, please, let me help. You're taking on too much with the work and the bookkeeping. I see the light under your door late at night when I get up to use the bathroom. There's no shame in getting help."

I turned the fire off under the sausages and forked one with vengeance. "There *is* shame in letting your mother do your work for you," I mumbled as the coffee pot spit and hissed. "I've got this under control." I forced a smile, then turned around to let her see how good and wonderful life was. She knew better, so did Dad, but it was Christmas, damn it, and my boyfriend was going to be here in less than eight hours. We had five days alone in a cabin with our college friends. It was going to be great. I had plans. Plans that involved me, Ryker, and the thin gold band hidden in my sock drawer. A band I'd been paying off in installments at Robinson's Jewelers in town for over a year. This holiday *had* to be perfect, even if the perfection was just an illusion until Ryker flew back to

Arizona with my engagement ring on his finger. I was not willing to accept anything less than a dream Christmas this year.

RYKER'S PLANE WAS LANDING. I FELT LIKE A KID ON Christmas Eve spying Santa dropping out of the clouds in his sleigh. There were two other people here at the Eden Crossing Airport. I knew them both, went to school with their kids, got into a fight with one when he'd called me a faggot and shoved me into a bathroom stall in my senior year. I'd cleaned that asshole's clock and gotten suspended for fighting and being theatrical.

Yeah, I was the one having homophobic slurs thrown at me while I was being hit, but I was the theatrical one.

Whatever. I'd kicked the shit out of Delbert Williams that day. Stupid, hateful jerk shouldn't have taken on a guy twice his size. I might've been gay, but I wasn't a tiny, tender thing like Hayne, my friend Scott's artistic boyfriend. You mess with the bull you get the horns, as my dad liked to say.

The plane rolled up to the terminal. I waited inside, pacing back and forth, my fingers itching to touch those damn curls of Ryker's. Disembarkation seemed to take forever, but suddenly there he was, jogging around the now-closed security station, his smile growing wider when his light brown eyes landed on me. He tossed his carry-on bag higher on his shoulder and broke into a dash that didn't stop until he was in my arms and my mouth was over his. Fuck the people gaping at the two gay boys kissing. To hell with what they thought. My man was finally back in my arms, and tasting his lips was the most important thing in the world.

"God, I missed you," I panted when we broke apart for air. Ryker slid his fingers into my short hair, then yanked my lips back to his. His tongue rolled over mine, teasing and tasting, making every nerve ending in my body fire off at once. Lust and love engulfed me. I began to edge him into a soda machine, but he snickered across my lips, then pulled back an inch or so, his lips pink and puffy from kissing.

"Easy, big man," he whispered, his fingernails gently raking over my scalp. "Your neighbors are going to call the cops on us."

I threw the six or so people gawking at us a dark look. They all lowered their eyes and scurried off, talking among themselves.

"Let's get out of here." I took his hand and tugged him away from the soda machine. My '89 Ford pickup sat out in the snowy parking lot. The new bright orange paint job that I'd given it last year in the hope of holding the rust at bay, made it stand out like a beacon among all the piles of freshly plowed snow.

"Why? Why that color, my man?" Ryker teased as he always did when he saw my truck. I bumped his hip with mine, took his bag, stowed it behind the seat, and then watched as he climbed up into her. His jeans pulled tight across his round, high ass. Skater ass, just like mine, just a little more compact. My dick was straining the zipper on my jeans. I was so happy that I'd had the sense to tell the guys to fly in tomorrow. Tonight was all ours. Mine and Ryker's. Alone. In the cabin overlooking the alfalfa fields.

I planned to do chores, eat dinner with the folks as they wished, and then cart Ryker to the cabin on my battered Polaris four-wheeler and not let him out of the big bed in the master bedroom until the next day. I pushed the boner with the heel of my hand. Ryker caught the movement and gave me a sultry wink that stole my breath.

He was fiddling with the CD player as soon as the engine cranked over. I slapped his hand, giving him a mock glower that he laughed off. Ah man, that laugh of his. It was so rich and warm, honest. The need to kiss him fired up. So I did.

"I love kissing you," he cooed, nipping at my lower lip before sitting back to buckle himself in. "Can we do some of my tunes?"

"There's no aux jack, babe," I reminded him. He huffed with such indignation it made me chuckle. "Welcome to Eden Crossing, population five hundred and two. Oh and dont forget the ten thousand cows."

"It's rustic, I know, but even people out here have to have cars with aux jacks for your phone, or Bluetooth, or even a damn antenna!"

"Maybe the people in town, but us poor farmers are lucky we can afford cans of spray paint to spice up our rides."

"Sorry, I was just being a dick, teasing a bit," he said. I shook my head, shaking away anxiety. "I love this old truck. Remember when we took her to that pond and dove off the tailgate into the water? Man, that was fun. Then afterward, we fucked in the back on that blanket that smelled like a barn. And the cows wandered up, and one licked your naked ass?" He laughed so hard at the memory that I had to join in.

"I will say that cow put your rimming skills to shame," I tossed out as we pulled away from the airport parking lot and onto a newly paved two-lane that would lead us to Eden Crossing proper. Ryker snorted at the chirp. He knew better. Delicate flakes floated down from a passing snow cloud. He chattered away the entire ride, which was about forty minutes each way, telling me about the team and his friends out in the Grand Canyon state.

"How's your dad doing?" he asked as Blake Shelton sang on about a girl he'd loved and lost.

"Muddling along. The orthopedic surgeon we dragged him to over in Dalton called back yesterday. Said that the X-rays of his hips are unlike anything he's ever seen. The left one is like the hip of an eighty-year-old, the right like a twenty-year-old. He asked Dad if he'd ever fallen, and of course he said no, but later that night, Mom told me about the time he fell off the back of a hay wagon when they were dating. Guess he was eighteen or so then. Said he landed on his hip and limped for a few days but never had it looked at, of course."

"Damn, so do you think he'll go get the surgery?"

I shook my head. "No money. We had to let the insurance lapse to pay the mortgage."

He was quiet for a moment, but I knew what was coming next. "I can help, Jacob." I shook my head. Ryker exhaled loudly. "I'm making pretty good money now. I can help. If it's not enough, I'm sure Dad and Ten would—"

"We don't need charity," I barked, my fingers curling

around the steering wheel. A snowplow passed us, blowing fine white powder onto the windshield.

"It's not charity; it's help. There's nothing wrong with asking for help, Jacob. I love you. Let me help."

"That's kind, and I love you for it, but the Bensons don't leech off their relatives, lovers, or the government. We have pride." I nodded at my own words, only to realize that they weren't my words at all. They were my grandfather's and my father's words. Still, they felt right. I was not going to let my superstar boyfriend pay for my father's hip replacement. There was no way in hell my dad would take a penny from Ryker, Jared, or Tennant, even if I did give in. "Can we not talk about this now? It's Christmas. You're here in Minnesota, and we have five whole days together. I want everything to be perfect."

"It will be," he said, reaching over to give my thigh a squeeze. "It's already perfect just because we're together."

I gave him a shaky smile. "It'll be even more perfect once we get home. Mom's making macaroni and cheese and homemade chicken tenders with her special ranch dip."

"*Yes!*" Ryker shouted, pumping the air while kicking at the floor of my truck. I prayed he didn't kick the floor out. The old girl was a little weak in spots.

When we pulled up in front of the farmhouse, Ryker was the first one out of the truck. My mother fussed over him, pushing his long curly hair from his face as Dad shook his hand and asked how the hockey was going. We spent the afternoon with my parents, did the evening chores, stuffed ourselves on Mom's mac n' cheese and tenders, and then around seven or so, we climbed onto my four-wheeler and rode off. The air was so cold it made my head hurt, but Ryker was behind me, holding on for dear life, his breath warm on my neck. We bounced and bounded over snow-covered fields where corn, oats, and alfalfa would be growing next summer. We splashed through the shallow creek that ran through our property, taking a deer trail that led into a thickly wooded area. The headlights on the Polaris illuminated the woods. A white-tailed doe raced across the path as we wound our way to the camp. When we came upon it, I throttled the four-wheeler down, then cut the engine. Smoke was pouring out of the chimney. I smiled at the kindness of my father to come out here to do that for us. He'd come a long way in his acceptance of his gay son hooking up with the rich boyfriend.

Ryker slid off the ATV, his bag on his back, and raced to the cabin. I followed hot on his heels, throwing the door open, spinning around to latch onto him, and then kissing him into the nearest wall.

"Bed… now," I panted over his slick lips.

"Yeah, yeah, bed now," he wantonly agreed, then kicked the front door shut. The only light came from the fire in the hearth. I'd never set eyes on a more beautiful sight than a passionate Ryker Madsen with the colors of a fire playing over his stunning face.

"Yeah, bed now." I took him by the hand and led him to the only bedroom with a double bed, clean sheets, and a tube of lube in the bedside drawer.

3

RYKER

Jacob had unbuttoned his jeans and was pulling them off before I'd even reached the bed, but I wasn't far behind, scrambling to keep up with him as he clambered onto the mattress and then reached over to grab the supplies that he'd dumped there.

I was mad with the need to touch him, and he'd taken up so much of my fantasies back home that to have him real and warm under me was intoxicating.

"It's been too long," Jacob growled, and all I could do was nod as I laid my weight on him and kissed his neck. "So fucking sexy when you got off that plane, and all I wanted to do was rip your clothes off and fuck you senseless in the damn airport."

We tussled for a moment, getting used to each other's weight, and then it was a chaotic madness of need and want, and Jacob's big body covering mine, was everything I ever wanted. I kissed him as if I was never going to see him again, savoring the taste of him and the texture of every part I could touch, the smoothness of his skin, the bristle of day-old stubble, the scent of shower gel, and the hard press of his cock against my thigh.

Jacob followed some unmapped path from my lips to my cheekbones and down to my throat, marking every inch of me with tiny nips and kisses, and I meant to move; I really did. I'd imagined this moment so many times, but all I could do was grip his flesh and hold on for the ride. There was no worry about the team or focusing on the game or planning and practicing and playing. There was nothing but the scent and weight of my boyfriend reminding me how much I'd missed him. I wanted him this way, I wanted to let go, I needed to, and the team and the game were nothing as I rode the sensation of being cared for and loved so utterly and completely. Jacob slid a little lower and paid a lot of attention to my nipples, his fingers on one, kissing and biting at the other, and I near lifted him from the bed. My nipples were hardwired to my cock, and I could feel Jacob's chuckle against my skin because he damn well knew that.

"I've missed this," Jacob growled, and I pushed against him, wanting more—desperate for more. "I want to go slow, but I can't..."

I finally moved, gripping him and yanking him to me as hard as I could.

"Not slow, not this time," I pleaded and felt for the lube, desperately trying to slick my fingers so I could push them inside me, but he was in my way, and he was fucking smiling, and all I wanted was him deep within me. I shoved him, spread my legs, and began to slick the way for him. His eyes widened as for a moment he watched, and then with another faintly territorial growl, he squeezed out more lube, and then it was both of us smoothing the way. We'd long ago forgone the need for a condom, and the image of him inside me, fucking me into the bed was more than enough for me to want to come right the fuck now. Jacob shoved and settled, pushing my thighs up. Then he kissed me as he pressed in slowly.

"Okay?" he asked, concern in the single word. It didn't matter how this madness to fuck fell on us. We would always look out for each other. I wiped my lube-sticky hands on the nearest T-shirt, then reached up and smoothed my fingers into his short hair. It was a little longer than he'd had it the last time we'd been together but it would never be as long and unruly as mine. I liked this hint of softness on my stubborn, sexy farmer.

"Always," I murmured and rocked back a little, his cock fully inside, his eyes wide and the kisses even deeper. I could come from this alone, just the gentle rocking, but Jacob took it higher, deeper, and my cock was trapped between us, so I rode the edge of an orgasm for the longest time. I didn't want it ever to stop. I wanted to stay in this moment forever, and tears threatened to fall with the perfect storm of emotions inside me. I loved Jacob. He was too far away, he was my everything, but I missed him so badly. I closed my eyes as he quickened his pace.

"I love you," he groaned as his movements stuttered, and I knew he was close. I yanked his head down in not such a pretty move. He opened his eyes briefly, and I was lost in the depths of his blue gaze.

"I love you," I told him back and slid a hand between us, circling my cock pressing against his belly, and when he roared his release, I was right there with him, a whiteout of sensation that seemed to last forever.

The kisses were frantic, then became lazier, and we lay quietly for a short while. I swore I'd never felt so much at peace as I did with Jacob softening inside me.

"I can't do this," he muttered between kisses. "I can't handle not seeing you, and not just to make love but to talk while we hold hands."

"It's killing me being apart," I told him the absolute truth of how I felt being away from him. Not because I wanted him to quit his life dramatically and follow me all over the fucking country, but because he *had* to know how much I loved him. Was I being selfish? Should I even have said something like that? Was this raw honesty too much to lay on him? All he did was sigh as he finally pulled out, then cleaned us up with what looked like wipes that were next to the bed. That was my Jacob, ready for everything. I gathered him close, and he rolled so that I lay half on him, my head tucked under his chin, and he tugged up a blanket to cover us. In that way we held each other, and I wanted this moment to last forever.

"Ryker? You still awake?" Jacob whispered into the softly lit room.

"Uh-huh."

"I've got something I wanted to say."

"Uh-huh."

"I love you so much."

I smiled against his skin, pressing a soft kiss at the base of his throat. "I love you too."

"It's been shit, you know, without you," Jacob murmured.

"It's been shit without you as well."

"But you have the team, and you're working to win, and…"

I couldn't help frowning. "And you have your farm, your legacy. You're the backbone of this country, right?"

He stayed silent for a moment. "The farm takes up everything in me, the work, the process, my plans for everything, tidying up this cabin so we'd have somewhere to stay, but life feels so gray when you're not here, like every day is just the same as the last. I don't know what I'm doing…"

I lifted my head and looked into his serious gaze.

"You were born to work a farm," I said, and even though a small treacherous part of me didn't want that to be right, it was the truth and part of his character, the heart of him that I loved just as much as the rest.

"Maybe it's not what…" He huffed a sigh and didn't finish the sentence, and I tightened my hold to show him support. "I'm tired," he added.

"Then sleep, because I'm right here. I've got you."

He wriggled a little to get comfortable, tucked the blanket close around us. "I've missed you too much. When I see the dawn or a shooting star or watch the leaves turn, I think about you and love you and miss you so damn much."

"And every time I get on the ice or listen to Tim McGraw, I miss you as well."

"Our ten-year plan is messing with my head," he admitted, and my chest tightened. Did he not want to stay with me? Was he not happy in this waiting game?

"It won't be for long. I'll play my years, stay healthy,

stay on task, retire in ten years, and move into this cabin with you, and then you'll never get rid of me."

He didn't say anything in return, but that was our unspoken strategy. I would play the game I loved, the one I was good at, and I would make my money, maybe lift the Stanley Cup. I would complete that part of my life to become financially stable, and then I would come home to Jacob, on his farm, and we could build a whole new life. Maybe even adopt some kids or do something else that was incredibly adult and right for us.

So what if the thought of this being all we had for the next ten years was an ache of regret that balled in my chest? We had our passions, him for his farming career, mine for hockey, and we had to make this work.

We lay in silence, but for some reason, sleep that normally followed making love with Jacob evaded me, and from the way Jacob's breathing hadn't evened out, I assumed he was awake as well.

"Dad's not been well," Jacob murmured.

"Yeah, you said he'd been in pain." I encouraged him to keep talking.

"Not just that. I see him try so damn hard to work, to scrape and scratch out a living, but the pain in him... and my mom, she looks so tired... is it worth it?"

That was the first time I'd ever heard Jacob imply that the farming life was wearing his family down. Although he was talking more about his parents, I couldn't fail to hear a hint of sadness in his voice. I wished he'd let me help his dad somehow, but I loved him as he was: stubborn, proud, and mine.

"Anything that matters to you is ultimately worth it," I

said and felt the most grown-up I'd ever been. Which was kind of a sad and worrying feeling when I wasn't sure I actually believed what I was saying. What if that *anything* that mattered meant that you were apart from the man you loved for so long?

He yawned then, and I snuggled just that few inches closer, and entwined as close as we could be, we slept.

THE NEXT DAY DAWNED BRIGHT AND COLD, AND FROST LEFT marks over cloudy windows and swirled patterns over the wood of the cabin. The fire had long since gone out, and my breath was a fog as I exhaled, but my extremities being chilled didn't matter because every part of me that touched Jacob was toasty warm.

"We should get up," he said when I moved against him. "Or at least, I need to get up. I have chores to take care of."

I let out a noise of protest and instead tugged the blankets up and over our heads until we were in a cocoon and I couldn't even see his face.

"Actually, we should hibernate until spring," I suggested.

Jacob's chuckle rumbled in his chest. "It's not like we need to eat or anything or use the bathroom or feed cows or play hockey. So yeah, we should stay right here until spring."

I pouted a little because my plan of never moving from this spot was a damn good one, albeit completely impractical. He laughed then because he'd know my expression and understand my need to just *be* with him. Because he knew *me*.

We scrambled out of bed, dressed quickly, thankful that the cabin seemed airtight because outside the windows was a winter vista so utterly beautiful and white that it chilled me to look at it. I loved snow, hell, I loved Christmas, always had, but I'd lived in a centrally heated house, not a cabin in the woods.

Jacob got a fire going in a gleaming chrome-and-iron log burner and pulled out various things from a cupboard, which mercifully, included coffee, and before long I was sitting next to the heat, curled up on a comfy chair, nursing coffee and nibbling on a warmed bagel. There were no Christmas decorations in here, not a tree or a single light. Nothing.

"We should get a tree," I announced, and Jacob side-eyed me as he pulled on a thick jacket.

"Okay."

"And decorations. On the way here you said we had a small generator, right? Well, we need to brighten the cabin up, make it look festive for the guys when they arrive, and maybe even get some lights."

"We could go when I'm done," Jacob agreed.

I turned a full three-sixty. As well as the door to the small bathroom and our room, there were two others, which I assumed would be where the guys would sleep when they got here. I already had images of the six of us crowded around the stove, the scent of pine filling the air from a rustically decorated tree, and the soft glow of Christmas lights making everything a hundred times more romantic.

"And we get a real tree?"

He frowned. "Like go to a lot and buy one?"

"Don't you have trees on your land?"

He tilted his head, and the frown was still there. "Yeah, I guess we do."

"Then when you get back, we'll go for the tree, and I can get decorations." Suddenly inspired, I leaped to my feet and started to pull on my jacket and boots. "Can I borrow your truck to get into town?" I knew that within twenty miles there were a couple of small towns, and one of them had to have a quaint little Christmas shop, right? After all, I'd seen all the movies, and those shops were everywhere.

"Hey," Jacob murmured as we stepped outside the door onto the gorgeous winter wonderland of his property and looked over the frozen lake with ice-heavy branches dipping low to nearly touch the ground. "I love you, Ryker," he said, and we kissed lazily for a moment before he tugged away.

"I love you," I said back, and then with one last kiss, we left the perfectly rustic cabin and headed off; he to his chores, and I to watch him for the longest time until I could set off on a mission to locate civilization, a shit ton of lights, and the tackiest decorations I could find.

If I didn't freeze to death on the back of his four-wheeler on the ride to the farmhouse first.

4

JACOB

MORNING CHORES WERE ROLLING ALONG WELL. DAD WAS up and going citing the high-pressure system that had moved into the region for his get-up-and-go. I suspected it was the anti-inflammatories he took twice a day. Without those, he'd not have been able to rise from his recliner. Still, it was nice to see him moving around the barn, even if his limp was pronounced. With the last of the cows now in their stanchions, I left Dad to go fire up the tractor and grab a couple of round bales from the hay barn. His hip prevented him from climbing onto the Massey-Ferguson. I peeled off my overalls in the mudroom, pulled on my work coat, and patted the small square lump in my front pocket. Ryker's ring. I'd slid it into my pocket yesterday, hoping for the ultimate romantic moment to propose. I'd thought maybe when we'd gotten to the hunting cabin, but things had sort of taken a sideways journey to sex and the moment to ask him to be mine forever never appeared. When would it, I had no idea, but I'd have the ring on me just in case.

I jogged around the lounging area, the cows who had been milked staring at me with big, demanding brown eyes.

"Yeah, yeah, I'm on it," I called to the Holsteins hurrying me along with their glowers. Cows were so pushy. Humming an old Randy Travis tune, I hustled into the equipment barn behind the twin silos and called a greeting to our new old tractor.

"Morning, Matilda," I said to the tractor, yanking the oil heater dipstick out and laying it aside on a worktable covered with old tractor parts. "Time to haul hay, old girl."

I climbed onto the tractor and rolled the engine over, smiling at how good I actually felt this morning, when a huge cloud of white smoke billowed out. The cloud rolled from the open door into the bitterly cold December morning.

"Fuck!" I snapped, quickly cutting the engine before jumping to the dirt floor. My old work boots hit the frozen soil with a *thud*. "This is so not what we need here, Matilda. Not today." Waving, I cleared the lingering wisps of smoke, then laid a hand on the dented hood that covered the ancient engine. Hoping it was something simple—and cheap—I began tinkering, checking for a leak or restriction in the suction line, then pulling off the fuel filter to see if it was plugged with dirt. When those didn't pan out, I checked the gaskets in case of a bad spray pattern. We'd once owned a Ford tractor where that had been an issue. The gaskets were clean and dry, and so I poked a bit longer, checking this and that until I concluded that we were looking at something larger than a dirty fuel filter.

"You been gone an hour, Jacob. Cows still need hay," Dad called, shuffling into the shed. "Is there a problem?"

"Yeah." I wiped my greasy hands on my jeans, then met his gaze. "White smoke is pouring out of her. I think it might be a bad injector or a dead cylinder, but I'll have to pull the engine to make sure."

"Shit." He sighed, placing a hand on the rusty red hood. "That's a big job."

"Yep."

"Well, let me get myself dressed, and we'll run to town."

"No, I'll go after I roll a few bales into the feedlot."

Dad gave me a nod, the despite my angry tirade about him helping, he got behind one of the six-by-six bales and helped me roll it, by hand, uphill to the lot where the cows were waiting impatiently. The sun was just now peeking over the tops of the barren trees.

"Jesus Christ, those sons of bitches are heavy," Dad panted. I wiped at the sweat running into my eyes. The single-digit temperature didn't feel quite as cold now. "We'll need at least four more, son."

I glanced at the sky, saw a crow passing overhead, and then bobbed my head.

It took us two hours to feed the cattle. I had to help my father back into the house, he was in so much pain. Mom fussed over him and got him into his recliner with a heating pad on his hip. I borrowed her keys and made a fast trip to Kennedy's Farm & Tractor on the other side of Eden Crossing, right by the Marston Creek. Jim Kennedy smiled at me when I entered. I returned the smile, and then we started talking. Ten minutes later, I wasn't smiling. In fact, I was close to tears.

"… parts for that old of a tractor are going to be impossible to find, Jacob. We can order you in a used engine, one that's been rebuilt, at a fair price." Jim looked up from the catalog of used parts and engines he'd flipped open. His gray eyes searched my face.

"What's a fair price?" I knew it would be far above the two hundred and three bucks remaining in the farm account.

"There's an 8.3 T diesel listed here in Kentucky for forty-five hundred dollars, minus the core charge. Core charge will add another thousand to the price. Then of course there's shipping. I'd say sixty-five hundred will cover it."

I closed my eyes, the smell of diesel fuel and oil sneaking into the showroom from the massive garage in the back making my eyes water. Yeah, that was it. The stink of gas was doing this to my eyes.

"We can't afford that. What about parts?" I asked, swallowing hard, then opening my eyes to study Jim's wrinkled face. He gave me a look of compassion. Our family had always shopped here for our farm equipment. The Bensons had worked the land for generations, and the Kennedys had kept our machinery working.

"Well, if it's a dead cylinder, you're looking at about two hundred and fifty for the cylinder itself, plus the new gaskets that you'll need to replace. We have a kit that has everything you'll need." He tapped away on a greasy calculator. I let my gaze travel over the new hay rakes and manure spreaders. "We're looking at about five hundred plus some odd change."

Gaze locked on that bright green hay tedder, I sighed internally. Actually, I may have screamed internally.

"Sure, okay. I have to make a run to the bank. Can you gather that kit up for me? I'll be back in ten minutes or so."

"Yep, can do." Jim gave me a kind smile that I had trouble returning. Stepping out into the cold, I walked to my mother's Malibu, dropped behind the wheel, and let the utter despair of the moment wash over me. A choked sort of gasp escaped. I hurried to tamp down the tears because honestly, what kind of man sits in a parking lot, crying over a fucking cylinder repair kit? Men took control and did what needed doing. With that mantra in my head, I pulled out onto the main road and drove to Eden Crossing, where I then sold the ring back to Robinson's Jewelers. The one I'd saved and scrimped for and sold my favorite dirt bike to buy. They were understanding and said they'd hold it until after New Year's just in case my fortunes changed. Pocket feeling as empty as my heart, I handed over all the cash in my wallet to Jim. The rest of my day was laid out before me, and it was nothing like I'd been dreaming it would be. Fucking life.

I took a break at lunch, stuffing some food into my face, then washing up to go get Ryker at the cabin. We had to pick up the guys at four. It was the last flight into the airport until after Christmas, which was in two days.

When I walked into the cabin, my face icy cold from the jaunt up there on the four-wheeler, I stepped into a world of holiday cheer.

"Hey! Hi!" Ryker bounced over to me, kissed me on the lips, then danced away with a string of garland in his hand. "So, I found out there are four of those dollar stores in or just outside of Eden Crossing."

I gave the room a once-over. It was hard to find an inch that wasn't festive. Even the plastic over the windows had been sprayed with that white flocking stuff. There were glittery paper balls and candy canes dangling from the ceiling, garland draped over all the window casings and across the mantel of the fireplace. Boxes and bags of trappings sat on the floor.

"Did you buy out all four stores?"

"Funny man. I love a funny man," Ryker replied with some cheek and a wink. "No, doofus, but I did have fun. Thanks for letting me borrow the truck. It's out back. I almost got stuck crossing the creek, but I wheeled her out of the deep part. Don't worry. I didn't drive on the hay fields and stayed in the path the four-wheeler made. Oh! Check it." He ran over to the mountain of bags and lifted one. "Stuff to make ornaments for the tree that we need to go get. I know we'll all be big-thumbed dorks, well, aside from Hayne, who will rock the shit out of the artsy stuff, but it'll be fun. And I packed *Cards Against Humanity*. Oh! We should grab some more snacks and some beer. Well, okay, maybe not beer because we're all athletes, and Scott is doing the clean and sober. Hey! Let's get some root beer and ice cream. Make floats and paint balls. Yeah, man, this is going to be *epic!*"

He wore his enthusiasm well. I wished I could match it. "Sure, sounds great, babe. My mom has some old lights she said we could borrow for the tree. I have the chainsaw strapped to the four-wheeler. If we're doing this tree thing, we better go and do it. We have to get the guys, and I still have to work on the tractor, so we can maybe do evening chores."

"Oh, is the tractor not working?" he asked, his cheeks pink from the fire, his light brown eyes glowing with good cheer.

"Yeah, but it's all good now. I ran to buy the parts and should have it chugging along by nighttime." I forced a smile that he returned; only his was a million watts brighter than mine. With a hoot of glee, Ryker bundled up and pulled me back outside. The sun on the snow blinded me, and I turned from the whiteness, slinging a leg over the four-wheeler, then scooting up so he could slide on behind me. He wrapped his arms around me, and off we went, the wind making our eyes leak, our noses run, and our cheeks as red as Santa's coat.

The farm pond was frozen solid as we roared past it. The perfect place for a shinny game when the guys were settled in. We rode through stands of naked oaks and elms, the recent snow heavy on the branches. Ryker would reach up as we passed and knock the snow off, making a cloud of dazzling diamonds on the air around us. When we reached the pines, I cut the engine, and we sat there, spellbound by the beauty around us. Tall evergreens coated with sparkling white powder, the flitter of a cardinal wing, the flash of a blue jay tail, and the whisper of the wind through the spruce were truly magical.

"It's so beautiful," Ryker whispered in my ear. I turned my head to gaze at him and found the surroundings paled in comparison.

"I love you so much, you know that, right?" I asked, and he grinned, the grin that he always bestowed on me when I confessed how much I adored him. The grin of a man who was truly loved. "I wanted to make this Christmas so special…"

"You have." He pressed his cold lips to mine, then climbed off the back, racing into the pines as he called to me over his shoulder to join him. Shaking my head when he began bellowing, "Where for art thou, oh most perfect Christmas tree?!" I loosened the bungee cords holding my dad's Jonsered to the rack on the front of the Polaris and loped off to join in the hunt for the most perfect tree. At least I could give him that.

He found the perfect tree with little fuss. It was a stumpy blue spruce with a space between the branches where a whitetail buck had scraped the velvet off his antlers, but Ryker declared it to be the one, and so with a swipe of the chainsaw, we felled our tree. Using a rope, we bound it tightly, then pulled it along behind us. Ryker sang carols the whole way home, and his off-key songs helped to lift the sadness in my heart, but only just a little. Knowing time was short, we propped the tree up beside the rickety front door of the cabin. Ryker jumped into my truck for the trip to the airport. Taking care to follow the path of the Polaris, he trailed me back to the farmhouse. Mom met us outside in nothing but a sweater.

"Dad's taking a hot bath to ease his hip. Then he's going to finish the tractor."

I glanced around Ryker at the house as if I could spy my father through the walls, a la Clark Kent. "Tell him to just rest, okay? I'll be back and will finish the job. Then I'll do chores. We'll have lots of help." She bit her lower lip. I pulled her into my arms for a quick hug. "Tell him to rest. I got this. I got it all, okay?"

"I'll try, but you know how he is." She chuckled thickly, giving my curious boyfriend a wobbly smile. "They're two peas in a pod when it comes to being bullheaded."

"Oh, trust me, Mrs. B., I am *well* aware," Ryker replied with sass. "We'll be back soon and with all kinds of help. Really, tell Mr. B. to just chillax. We're all up for mucking out cow poop!"

She snickered, as did I. I kind of suspected Benoit, Scott, Hayne, and Ethan really had no desire to wash off teats or shovel cow manure. They were city boys, like Ryker. I adored them all but they didn't know a dairy milking cluster from a marble cake.

Should prove to be an interesting evening in the milking parlor.

5

RYKER

I COULD NEVER HAVE IMAGINED A WORSE SCENARIO THAN five men in a cow barn who shouldn't have been anywhere near the barn or the animals. Everything started okay. I mean, we all listened intently to what we were being told, but maybe I wasn't listening as closely as I could have been, because I couldn't stop staring at the way Jacob's lips formed the words 'teat dips' and 'important'. It was me who fucked up first, tripping over a shovel, and it was Scott who got the brunt of my stupidity and ended up face planting in cow shit. Add in Hayne completely losing it and crying with hysterics as Jacob's mom marched Scott off for a shower, and I thought maybe we'd reached our limit on stupidity.

How wrong could one man be?

A cow kicked out at Ethan, who jumped back and flattened a newly clean Scott, right back into the shit, and what had been kind of funny the first time around now descended into halfhearted recriminations that were in danger of becoming more, as we were tired and cold.

Friendship and camaraderie stopped at the level of cow shit, it seemed.

This was *not* the way I'd envisioned us all joining together and helping Jacob. Things were certainly not the way I wanted this Christmas get-together to start.

In the end, Jacob sighed, thanked us all so politely that it put Benoit the Canadian to shame, and ushered us all out into the snow, with Scott plodding back to the house, Hayne scampering after him, torn between laughter and sympathy, and the rest of us deciding to wait for them before heading out.

It was dark, freezing, but we bundled up and waited, and I really had hoped it would be all six of us who went to the cabin.

"I've got some last chores to handle," Jacob announced as we were getting ready to leave. I didn't know if it was his tone of voice or the half smile he gave me, but there was something wrong, or rather, there was something *off* with my boyfriend. Earlier, he'd been cheerful to get the tree with me, and if not happy, then he'd at least indulged my need for a tree. He hadn't been angry that I'd made the cabin into a dollar store wannabe Aladdin's cave, and he'd enjoyed exchanging frosty kisses, but this afternoon he'd been...

Wrong.

The Jacob today versus the Jacob from yesterday was like the man I'd known just before his final exams, the one who wouldn't admit to anyone that he was scared to fail and only gave in and shared his fears when I found him nearly-catatonic, staring at a textbook in the library. I resolved to talk to him later, but it wasn't the time. For now, it was my job to make sure that Scott, Hayne, Benoit, and Ethan all made it to the cabin alive. It was certainly a cozy trip. Hayne sat on Scott's lap, holding on for his life, his hood falling down, and his curls bouncing as we passed over every hole and lump under the snow. Ethan was wedged by the door, humming under his breath nervously, and Benoit sat in the back, the only one whooping at every dip and dive while gripping bags and a selection of hockey gear. Crazy-ass goalie. We at least made it to the cabin in one piece, a combination of me following what trail I could see in the headlights and the fact that the old truck seemed indestructible.

We lost Hayne immediately, with Scott stumbling after him, vanishing into the trees.

"Oh my god," Hayne said on repeat. "I need my paints… this is just…"

We left them to it, the rest of us heading into the cool cabin. Jacob had shown me how to start the stove, and that was my priority. Then I lit the small lanterns in the food prep area and finally turned back to face Ethan, who appeared to be struck dumb with shock, and Benoit, who grinned so widely I thought it must've hurt. At their feet was a tumble of bags and sticks, and Ben had already taken off his huge thick coat, then taken out one of his jerseys and pulled it over his sweater. I *could* tease him about the team, but anyone who played on the Raptors had no place teasing anyone about anything. Nope, I knew it was going to be everyone else explaining to me, nicely of course, about how shit the Raptors were. I seriously didn't have to be told that. Only I also felt incredibly protective of my team because we'd begun to bond a little. Not much, but enough now that Aarni was gone that there was *some* cohesion in play. After all, I was part of the hottest line in Raptors history. Not that this was saying much.

"Tell me there's a pond, and that it's frozen over and we can get out there tomorrow." Benoit demanded, and side-eyed Ethan

His enthusiasm was infectious. "Oh yeah, there's a pond, a big one, solid ice," I explained, and we exchanged high fives.

"What is"—Ethan waved at the ceiling, the dangling cheap-ass decorations twisting in the multitude of tiny breezes that came in through cracks, and the rising heat from the stove—"… this?" he finished.

"Christmas!" Ben exclaimed and hurried over to the tree, poking at it and twisting it slightly. "Perfect," he announced and then yanked Ethan closer. "Look at that bit there. I bet some animal rubbed close to the tree and took off the growing part. Look," he was demanding and pointing at the bare spot that I loved, and finally Ethan seemed to relax, which I think was helped by Benoit kissing him soundly.

Cue the arrival of a frozen-to-the-core Hayne, who carefully placed a box on the table and flicked it open, pulling out a smallish canvas, one of five I counted, and then spread out his paints. He did all of this while we watched, all of us knowing better than to interrupt his artistic flow, even though we'd lost the table for now. I knew that the scent of the oils and the splashes of color in his hair would be a sensory reminder of us all living together in Owatonna, and I craved that connection as much as I craved candy.

We independently bundled everything into the two other rooms, neither as big as ours but both with solid beds and mattresses that I'd sent money to Jacob for. He'd wanted to argue with me, even over FaceTime I could tell that, but when I pointed out that it was entirely my idea to get us all together rather than have the cozy twosome he'd suggested at first, he'd backed down. Damn, stubborn man.

I showed everyone where things were, which took all of ten seconds, and then we left Hayne painting away, and the four of us piled into Ethan and Benoit's room, sprawled on their bed passing Cheetos around and drinking hot coffee, sharing memories, shooting the breeze. But even though I loved seeing them, all the while I listened out for Jacob coming in.

Everyone had reluctantly gone to bed before he turned up, and I'd wavered from worry to annoyance that he had to stay out so late to work, and then the minute I saw him I felt such love that I stumbled a little, right next to Hayne's icy masterpiece, which he'd propped up to dry.

"Jeez, are you okay?" Jacob asked me with concern.

"Me?" I thumbed my chest and went to his side, cradling his cold face, pausing to push his hood down and pull off his beanie, flattening his hair which spiked up comically. "You're so cold." I took off his gloves and held his icy hands in mine, then tugged him toward the stove. "Why were you so long?"

"Extra time," he joked. "You know what it's like."

I helped him out of his coat, which was damp with

snow, and hung it close enough to the stove that I hoped it would be dry by the morning. Then I made him sit on the chair, and pulled out the stove kettle to boil water and make the best hot chocolate I could without milk, whipped cream, or marshmallows. We didn't talk while I did that; I let him have his peace as he appeared oddly reserved and mesmerized by the flames in the stove.

My instincts told me something was wrong, but maybe now wasn't a good time to ask if everything was okay. What if a cow had died? What if a shit ton of milk had soured? Not that this was likely. After all, it was as freezing out there as a goddamn refrigerator. But what if he'd just overworked himself to the point that he couldn't move at all? I shuffled a chair close to him and handed him his chocolate.

"Drink this," I demanded. "It will warm you up."

"Did everyone get in here okay?" he asked after a few moments of sipping the hot drink, and I wondered if maybe he was thawing from the inside out.

"Hayne did art, Scott was in charge of handing him paints, Benoit poked at the tree, and I really think Ethan went into shock, muttering something about the Bahamas. Not that I was entirely listening. Then we sat around and talked hockey, about all the college games we played when it was about the sheer honest fun and not just work. That was all good."

He looked at me over the rim of his mug. "Are you not having fun with the Raptors, then? I thought that was the point of you having the career you dreamed about?" I couldn't make out his tone, and I blinked at him. Was that some kind of criticism or...? "Sorry," he apologized immediately. "What I meant to say was I hope that you're enjoying your work with the Raptors. It just came out wrong."

Very wrong. Yet another indicator that things weren't entirely on an even keel here.

I held his free hand and squeezed it to reassure him.

"I love what I'm doing," I reassured him. "I've always wanted it, and yeah, it's not easy sometimes, but I wouldn't switch what I'm doing for the world."

There. Was that enough reassurance to quiet his fears that I wasn't happy? I hoped so because I assumed he was worrying about me. He did that a lot.

He smiled then and shook off my hold, taking his mug to the tiny sink and putting some water in it to soak.

"I'm really happy it's going well for you," he said with his back to me. I crossed over to stand behind him, sliding my arms around his middle.

"I love you so much," I murmured, kissed that space between his shoulder blades, and inhaled the scent of my man, who'd worked so hard. He turned in my hold and looked down at me, cradled my face in his large hands and kissed me so deeply it took my breath away.

"I love you more," he announced, then winked at me, and just like that, calm, happy Jacob was back, and I laced my hands around his neck and held on tight.

"Want to go to bed?" I lowered my tone and waggled my eyebrows.

With a contented sigh, he pulled me close. "Yeah. Always."

.   .   .

When I woke up, Jacob was gone, but I knew that was going to be the case. For such a big guy, he had this way of moving silently around places and always refused to wake me up when we were together. I was disappointed because I kind of wanted to be woken up, just so I could hug the warmth of him, all sleepy and cozy in bed, but instead I woke up to his cold side and the chatter of my friends outside in the main part of this tiny cabin. When I joined them, it was to see Ethan in charge of breakfast, which mainly consisted of bagels, pots of cream cheese, bacon bits that were fairly unrecognizable as such, chocolate, jelly, coffee, and a pile of confectionary that had come from god knows where. Hayne had cleared half of the table, but we didn't stand on ceremony, and I actually ended up eating my body weight in bagels while sitting cross-legged on a cushion by the stove. I had to hand it to Ethan. He was one bossy fucker, but he really knew his way around this makeshift cabin-in-the-snow kind of thing.

Turned out Ethan was also in charge of the snowman, which according to Ben was something we *had* to do. Working as a team, we ended up with a close approximation of a yeti-sized shape next to the cabin, using some of the cheap Christmas decorations to make him look handsome. Ethan's words, not mine.

"Yep, that is one gorgeous snowman," Ben teased Ethan, which somehow meant we ended up in a snowball fight, Hayne passing on the game and heading inside to paint, and Scott and me against Ben and Ethan.

"This is not a fair fight," I announced when Ben dodged a volley of snow we'd catapulted at him. He was way too fast and slick at avoiding us, but it seemed Scott and I were as devious as each other, calling Uncle on the fight and then shoving Ben into a hole and pelting him from the top.

Tired, happy, and laughing, we headed back inside, water hot, coffee on, just in time for Jacob to appear again. He seemed happier this morning, high-fived and hugged everyone, listened to our stupid snowball stories, and even complimented our weird-ass snowman. Also he had a rucksack of decorations that he'd brought back with him, which included the lights he'd mentioned, large colored bulbs on thick cord, and a collection of glittery things that his mom said would suit the cabin.

I rummaged through the bag, finding treasure after treasure, laying the lights out to see if they worked, and then I found something that made my heart fill with emotion. Made of two wooden pegs and painted cardboard, with a fluffy woolen nose in bright scarlet, it was clearly a homemade Rudolph, and when I turned it over in my hand, I saw a scrawl that said *Jacob*.

"Oh wow." I handled it like the precious object it was, part of the childhood of the man I'd fallen in love with, and my chest grew even tighter. I knew that my dad had a collection of the stuff I'd made as a kid, he and Mom both, but I hadn't seen any of it for a long time, and anyway, those were my creations. This was Jacob's past I had in my hands, and it was special.

"I was six," Jacob said and reached out to touch it with a soft smile. "I remember my mom cried when I brought it home and that she put it right at the front of the tree, made this huge fuss about what I'd done. Every Christmas

it came out, but for the last couple of years, we haven't…
yeah."

He didn't finish the sentence, and abruptly that wistful
sadness was back, which I attempted to kiss away.

"Get a room!" Scott announced and jumped on us.

"Asshole," I yelped and shoved him away, holding the
peg reindeer protectively to my chest.

"What you got there?" Scott asked and peered at my
hand, but for some reason, I didn't want him to see. I
wanted it to just be me and Jacob and the tiny reminder of
him as a boy, and I didn't want it ruined.

"Nothing to do with you," I snarked and pushed him
again, which as usual ended with us wrestling, me one-
handed until Jacob helped me out and the whole thing
finished with me and Jacob both sitting on Scott, laughing
so hard we were crying.

Hell, it was good to have everyone here.

6

JACOB

THEY SAID THEY WANTED A SHINNY GAME, AND SO THEY were getting one. Just as soon as I got the tractor engine put back in place. I breathed a sigh of relief when it was settled and off the engine hoist. Hours of work lay ahead yet, but things were looking good. Maybe we could avoid rolling hay bales through snow and ice and cow shit today. What a novel idea!

Wood stove roaring in the corner, I gathered up my tools and got to work. I'd moved away from my warm boyfriend at quarter after two, leaving him and everyone else sound asleep to come here to wrap up this job. I'd filled a thermos with disgusting instant coffee, skipped eating, and crept out the front door, wishing against wish I could stay in bed, cuddle with Ryker, and enjoy Christmas morning, just this one time. But cows do not milk and feed themselves. There's no such thing as a day off for people who care for animals. No vacations either. We had never had family holidays like so many other kids did. No trips to Disney World. There was no one to tend to the cattle, and we simply couldn't afford it. That trip to Canada where I'd met Ryker had set us back financially. I thought, when the nights were cold and long and sleep eluded me, that even with a small bursary, the trip had been another step the money issues we now were buried under.

I refused to dwell on the ring. I'd have to come up with something else to give Ryker, but I had no idea what. It was Christmas Day. I had nothing for the man I loved. Nothing. Unless he could enjoy the sounds and sight of a working tractor, he'd get nothing from me. It made me sad and mad, both emotions vying for that gold medal. Right now, anger was winning. As I worked and ratcheted and skinned my knuckles more times than I could count, my resentment for this damn tractor and this farm grew. By the time my mother, dressed for morning chores, arrived with more coffee and an egg sandwich wrapped in foil, I was seething.

"Take a break and eat, son." She walked over to me, holding out the food and drink. I waved her off. "Jacob, you have to eat. Now take five minutes and—"

My greasy fingers slipped off the wrench, and my knuckles raked over the engine block. Again. This time I didn't just cuss. I whipped the wrench across the equipment shed and rounded on my mother. It was ugly. *I* was ugly.

"Jesus Christ, Mom, I don't *have* five minutes! I don't have one minute! This fucking farm is sucking every second of my life away from me. I don't even have time to spend with my friends or my boyfriend because of this miserable place. So stop trying to make me feel better because there *is* no feeling better until I can get this fucking tractor running and do chores!"

She stood there, chin high, eyes dewy, shoulders back, the lines in her face that she shouldn't have at such a young age deep as she glowered up at me.

I lowered my eyes to my bloody knuckles. "I'm sorry, Mom, so sorry. I don't know where that came from. I just…" I glanced at her. The anger was still lingering in her jaw, but her blue eyes were softer now. "It's Christmas, and I don't have anything for Ryker. How do I face him? He'll have gifts for me, the guys will all have gifts for each other, and there I'll stand, stinking of cow shit and grease, with nothing but a measly apology to give him. There are days I *hate* this farm. I hate being poor. I hate working on secondhand equipment all the time. I hate not knowing if the milk check will cover the two mortgages. I just…" I ran out of venom then and dragged myself to the rear of the shed to pick up my wrench. Unable to look at her, I went to work.

"You will look at me, Jacob Benson," she said after a moment of utter silence passed. A green log in the stove cracked like a pistol. I lifted my gaze from the engine and looked right at my mother. "You are *never* to speak to me in that tone of voice ever again, nor are you to use that kind of language in my presence. Do not *ever* think that you're too big for me to wash your mouth out with soap. Do you understand me, young man?"

"Yes, I understand. I'm sorry. I am. I didn't mean to talk that way." I rolled the greasy wrench around in my hand as I spoke. Her tight jaw loosened slightly. "It's just that life is so hard. Nothing we do seems to get us ahead.

And I miss Ryker. When he's gone, it's like this gaping raw wound in my chest. I just…" I pulled it together. "I'm just upset that this tractor is taking all my time, that's all. Don't think on it anymore."

"What happened to the special gift you were saving for?" She jabbed the sandwich and thermos at me. When I took the coffee, she lifted the wrench from my other hand. "Eat, drink. I'll get the spark plugs back in."

With a bob of my head, I peeled back the foil and took a big bite. Cheese and bacon bits hit my tongue, the flavor a favorite one of mine. Mom made the best egg sandwiches in Minnesota.

"So, the gift for Ryker," she prompted, lifting a spark plug up to the overhead light to eyeball the gap. Farm girls rock.

I swallowed after another bite. "I sold it to pay for the parts we needed for the tractor."

Her blue eyes widened in shock. "Why didn't you tell us?"

"There isn't enough money in the farm account to cover the cost of the kit."

She worked the inside of her cheek, the spark plug lying in her palm for a second before she dropped it into place and reattached the cover.

"What was it you had bought for him?" She was tentative, and I was beaten.

"An engagement ring."

"Oh, Jacob," she gasped, her voice filled with pain, just as my heart was. I shook my head, hoping to dash away the tears that welled up. Instead of crying or looking at her, I focused on my sandwich. Mm-mm, it was good. Fuck. "Look at me, Jacob."

"I really can't right now, Mom, please…"

She padded over to me, her fingers slick with gasoline and grease. I peeked up from the last bite of fluffy yellow egg and Velveeta to witness her removing her anniversary band from where it sat atop her wedding band and engagement ring.

"No, Mom, no," I said with as much force as I could muster. "That was from Dad for your twentieth anniversary." It wasn't an expensive ring, not like some you see. It was just a skinny white gold band with diamond chips all round it. Dad had saved up for a year to buy it, and she adored it. Said it made her feel like a duchess.

"And now I'm giving it to you to give to Ryker." She held out the band between two thin work-worn fingers.

"No, it's yours. And it's too small. That will never fit him. And it's a woman's ring. The band I got him was thicker, manly, and engraved."

"This is engraved, although I reckon the lettering is worn off by now. And as for it being a woman's ring, since when are promises to love each other forever male or female?" She shook the ring again, the itsy-bitsy diamonds glinting in the ugly glare of the old work lamps overhead. "Take it and give it to him. Tell him it has sentimental value because it was your mother's and she gave it to you to bestow upon the person who won your heart. He can wear it on his pinkie or around his neck on a chain until you can buy back the ring you got him."

"I don't think so. It's not… it's not *his* ring."

"Jacob, the ring is just a symbol, honey. It's the love in two people's hearts that's important, that binds the couple together. The rings and the other fancy wedding stuff is just that. Stuff. I don't have much to give you, but I can give you this. Please, take it."

There was no way I could eat now or drink, so I coughed and sputtered, took the tiny ring from her, slid it into my wallet for safekeeping, then swept her into my arms and cried into her hair as she patted my back and whispered soft, motherly things.

"I love you so much," I said after the mushy moment passed.

"And I love you. Now, let's get to work here. If we stop fiddling around, we might have this done in time for you to get back to the cabin and my future son-in-law." She patted my cheeks and kissed the tip of my nose, just like she'd done forever.

"He might not say yes," I warned her.

"I've seen the way that young man looks at you. He'll say yes. Now, pass me the rest of the spark plugs, and you work on something else."

"Yes, ma'am." I smiled the first real smile in days and handed her the spark plugs.

When I returned to the cabin, none of the guys were moving. It was after eight, and no one had stirred. So I pulled off my boots, hat, gloves, and coat, threw them onto the sofa, and slipped back into the master bedroom. There lay Ryker, long powerful legs spread wide under the covers, his arms over his head, face buried in his pillow. I shucked off my clothes quietly and slid under the blanket, keeping an inch or so between the radiant heater that was my boyfriend and my cold self. He grunted a bit when I leaned over him, settling my chest to his back. When I kissed along his shoulder, he purred like a cat with a belly full of smoked salmon. When I shoved my icy fingers under the waistband of his sexy blue briefs, he sucked in a breath.

"Fuck, dude! Really, your hands are freezing!" he yelped, wiggling to get away, but I leaned in over him, placing more of my weight on his back as I worked my hand between his ass cheeks and found his hole. He stopped trying to get away, rising off the bed, encouraging me to play more. So I did. I tasted his back and the nape of his neck as I worked a spit-covered finger into him. His hips moved sinuously. I pressed deeper, finding that knot of nerves that made him shudder and whimper my name.

"Merry Christmas, baby," I panted beside his ear as I worked him into an orgasm that left him sweaty, weak, and unable to speak. Then as gently as possible, I moved him over, captured his mouth, and licked deep, pulling sweet soft sounds from him as he ran his palms over my arms and back. I didn't have to ask for him to please me. He was eager to do so, taking me in hand, pulling and tugging and stroking while he whispered tender things to me, things that made me buck and groan when I tumbled over the edge, things that eased me deeper into our love, things that would never be repeated outside of our bed.

"So yeah, hell of a present." Ryker chuckled afterward, his sticky hand resting on my belly, his curls damp with sweat. I rolled to my side to study him. He was breathtaking lying beside me, the winter sun on his flushed face, the smell of us thick on his skin.

"I love you," I told him, reaching up to tug a curl. He kissed my throat, murmuring that he was devoted to me as well. I thought to ask him to marry me then. I even moved to go get the ring from my wallet when someone pounded on the door.

"Time for hockey!" Benoit roared, slapping the floor with what could only be a stick. "Stick taps for the free porn soundtrack too."

"Asshole!" Ryker and I both yelled, but my man's cheeks were red as a candy apple.

I scrambled over him, pinning Ryker to the bed. There was so much I wanted to say to him, but the time to propose had passed, so I'd have to wait for another perfect moment.

"We better get out on the ice before Ben breaks down the door."

And so we left the cocoon of our bed for the bitter cold of a Minnesota farm pond at eight a.m. on Christmas morning. The air was so cold my nose hairs froze. Our breaths clouded in front of us, and steam rose from our knitted caps.

It was a pretty loose game, with only one net and one goalie, but we had a blast. Ethan and I were defending Benoit from Ryker and Scott. Hayne had no interest in strapping on skates, but he was on the sidelines cheering and sipping from the thermos of coffee he'd brought along.

Ryker was good. Damn good, fast and quick, his skill set noticeably above Scott's, who was no slouch. But Scott hadn't played professionally as Ryker did. Neither did I. Ethan had, but that was behind him now. Hell, Ethan had retired and had a leg that was probably aching like a bad tooth in this cold. But he was a hockey player, so he kept his pain to himself.

Ryker tried a fancy deke on Ben, but the young goalie was too damn fast.

"What do you call that move? My mother's got more flair!" Ben called out.

Ryker flipped him off, then picked up the puck. I settled into a stance, low, weight balanced on my skates, eyes flickering between Scott and Ryker as they shuttled the puck back and forth between them while they inched closer to the goal. Ryker gave me a wink, then pulled this Tennant Rowe spin-a-rama move on Ethan that left Ben wide open. I threw myself in front of the slapshot, the puck catching me in the chest, then dropping to the ice. Scott and Ryker dove on it, sticks clacking as I rolled to my belly to pin the puck. And there I lay, like a massive log, laughing at the names the two forwards were calling me.

"Okay, someone blow the fucking whistle! This is a blatant delay of game tactics!" Ryker bellowed to Hayne. "Ref! What's the call?" We all looked at Hayne. He gaped at us, his bright pink mittens wrapped around his cup of coffee, the wind throwing his wild curly hair into his face.

"Oh, uhm, the call is he who lies on the puck owns it. Is that right?" Hayne shouted back, and we all laughed.

Scott skated over to the edge of the pond for a quick kiss from Hayne, which turned into a much longer kiss, which meant that we had to pelt the two who were sucking face with snowballs. Hayne hid behind Scott, who was trying, and failing, to Mickey Mantle each ball of snow whipped at him out into centerfield.

Ethan called an end to the impromptu madness. "To quote Roger Murtaugh, 'I'm too old for this shit', and my balls are frozen solid. Let's go inside, eat, open presents, and watch some of those DVDs we brought up."

"*You* brought up," Ben said, his mask in his hand. "None of us own a DVD."

Ethan looked at each of us. We all shook our heads.

"Christ, I *am* fucking old," Ethan lamented.

"I love you anyway, Gramps," Ben teased, pulling his fiancé in for a hug and a smooch.

Dropping an arm around Ryker's neck, I stole a kiss as well. He beamed at me, his love so evident it made me feel unworthy in so many ways. Here I was with nothing to offer him but a used white gold band and a farm on the verge of bankruptcy. And there he stood looking at me as if I hung the moon and stars. I hugged him and just held him until the guys shouted at us to get moving before Ethan's old balls got any colder.

"You okay?" Ryker asked. I nodded, brushed a soft little snowflake from his hair, and led him back to the cabin.

"As long as I have you in my arms, yeah, I'll be okay."

"*DIE HARD* IS *NOT* A CHRISTMAS MOVIE," BEN STATED FOR the third time, his eyes rolling so dramatically that I swore they were about to pop out of his head. He was actually the only one in the *Die Hard*-isn't-a-Christmas-movie camp, the rest of us saying it was. Well, all except Hayne, who shrugged and continued with his drawing. He was lost in sketching each of us as a Christmas gift, and I couldn't wait to see what he made of it.

"Hush, you." Ethan pulled him in for a noogie, and they wrestled like idiots until they ended up on the floor and Ben was yelling Uncle. "Say '*Die Hard* is the perfect Christmas movie', and I'll let you up."

Ben could've easily bucked him off, but part of me thought he enjoyed being squashed flat by Ethan.

"No, I won't say—" He stopped talking when Ethan bounced a little and then tickled him more.

"Say it, or die," Ethan growled.

Ben wriggled. "How can you say that? What's

Christmassy about a film where everyone dies and a building gets blown up? Back me up here, Hayne!"

Hayne glanced up from his sketch pad and blinked at Ben, looking confused to see Ben and Ethan on the floor.

"Huh?"

"*Die Hard* is not a Christmas movie, right?" Ben called up and snorted when Ethan tickled him some more.

Hayne clearly wasn't in the room with us right now, a smudge of blue on his cheek and streaks of scarlet in his hair. "Is that what you're watching?" he asked and peered at the screen, just as Bruce Willis, in his tatty white vest, put an office chair packed with explosives down an elevator shaft. The movie cut to a wide-angle shot of an entire floor of the Nakatomi Plaza building exploding, and Hayne winced. Then he just let out a soft "hmmm" before looking back down at his sketch pad.

Scott pressed a kiss to his boyfriend's curls and shifted a little to make sure Hayne was still comfortable on his lap. "What Hayne meant by that is that I get his vote, and I say that *Die Hard* is definitely a Christmas movie."

"Say it." Ethan was laughing so hard with Ben that Ben's squeaked words were difficult to make out, enough so he could deny he'd even said it.

"Okay, okay, it's a Christmas movie! Now let me up!"

"Word," Ethan said and leaned over to high-five Scott before helping Ben to his feet. It couldn't just have been me who saw he had his fingers crossed.

"To be fair, there is Christmas music," I added and then pushed my phone back under my sweater attempting to recall what I'd just read. "Also, it's set during the holiday period, in fact, on Christmas Eve itself. There is a salvaged romance, cheesy lines, and at one point John McClane even goes down an elevator shaft, which is a symbolic chimney, so you know, it's Christmas."

Everyone barring Hayne stared at me, and I couldn't help the twitch of my lips nor the squeal I let out when Jacob started tickling me. Which of course led to Scott joining in, meaning Hayne had to lift his sketch pad out of the way to save it, and Ethan dying from laughter as he attempted to stop Ben from getting hold of the big old laptop we were all huddled around. Jacob pretended to help me, but in the end he was the one holding me so he was going to get what was coming the next moment his guard was down.

None of us were really watching the film, Hayne drawing, Scott watching Hayne. Ben was grumbling about the difference between *Die Hard* and his personal favorite, *Elf*. Ethan was trying to watch the film, same as me, but from the way his mouth moved, he was whispering lines before they happened, just to annoy Ben, I guess he'd seen it as often as I had. *Die Hard* was one of my dad's favorite films, and for a moment I felt a familiar twinge of regret that I wasn't seeing him or Mom today. It wasn't the first time I'd felt that, but it didn't last long, though, because Jacob curled his fingers into my hair and tugged me in for a kiss.

"What're you thinking about so seriously?" Jacob asked, pressing his thumbs into my neck, where I was clearly tense.

"The future," I blurted and then wished I could take it back because it wasn't only Jacob who heard me.

"What about it?" Scott asked, which drew the attention of Ethan, who glanced away from the film.

"Nothing, just watch the Christmas movie," I said.

"It's not a—" Ben started, but Ethan shut him up with a hard kiss that carried on for so long that Scott and I threw chips at them.

"What about the future?" Jacob asked when Ethan and Ben finally broke apart, and Ethan cleared up the chips.

"Nothing. Not really. Okay, well, yeah…"

"Use your words," Jacob said drily.

"Just thinking about not seeing Mom or Dad over Christmas but how it actually feels okay because I'm not a kid anymore, and you and I will be making our own traditions, and passing things down to our family one day, like my love of *Die Hard* and your mom's Christmas lights." We'd strung the lights in the porch, out of the blasts of frozen air and the swirling snow, and I could see the warmth and glow of them through the scuffed window. I loved that they were a part of Jacob's past, a gift from his mom that we could take anywhere we wanted.

"You forget we can pass your hockey sticks from Ten down through the generations," Jacob deadpanned, "and my entire collection of *Star Wars* figures."

"Wait, you have a collection of *Star Wars* figures?"

Jacob smirked at me. "Doesn't every small kid?"

"Not me. I collected NHL trading cards."

"Of course you did." Jacob pressed a kiss to the tip of my nose. "And I bet you had loads of them signed personally by friends of your family, right?"

"Okay, so I knew people, who knew people." I decided not to tell him about my Gretsky collection, or the rare early Lemieux card, and it was my turn to smile then. "Anyway, they're my pension."

"Jesus, guys, stop talking about getting old and shit," Scott interjected. "You're seriously harshing the *Die-Hard-don't-care* buzz we had going on."

"We all need to have some plan for the future," Ethan said primly, and Ben's snort of laughter was so loud that all of us, even Hayne, started to laugh. Of course, Ben's derision of Ethan's sensibleness, if that was even a word, led to more of them kissing, which necessitated more chip throwing. Finally, after it all died down, something changed in the room, a seriousness that was always a scheduled part of any of us getting together.

"You know something?" Ben started. "I've never thought about life after hockey, apart from the fact that I'll be with Ethan." Ethan made a cute little *awwww* sound and hugged Ben. "What about your future? What will you do after you finish with hockey?" Ben was completely focused on me and whatever answer I gave him, and that really put me on the spot.

Why did I even think of talking about the future today? No one needed to think ahead when they could've been enjoying the moment. If I was really honest, apart from being with Jacob, I hadn't thought that far ahead. I was trying to make my way with the Raptors, and of course, a family with Jacob was my entire future, in that he featured in every part of it. I wanted him there when I won my first trophy, when the team made it to the Cup finals, when we won that Cup, when I was getting to the end of my career and became the old-timer to the younger kids on the team. In every part of my future,

Jacob was right there, celebrating my successes, looking on me fondly as I made my mark. Likewise, I would be there for him, with every little thing he did on his farm, when he took it over and made it better than it could have ever been without him, when he raised the perfect cow, if that was a thing, or when his farm won an award for the most amazing milk ever produced in Minnesota. All the way through, my future was me, Jacob, and a whole heap of successes born from our hard work and constant love.

"Coach maybe? Like Dad?" I said in simple terms. "Find a team close to here and do that." I glanced up at Jacob, who was focusing very hard on me. "We can build that house we talked about, Jacob, the one with the pond and the hot tub, and then all you guys can come visit us at Christmas and in the summer." I waited for Jacob to agree, but he changed the subject.

"What about you, Ben? What will you do?"

Ben glanced at Ethan. "Travel all over Canada, to all the tiny nooks and crannies, all the way up to the ice, and over to Vancouver Island, see some bears on Prince Rupert Island." He seemed to be looking for something from Ethan. "Adopt some kids, make a family."

Mine sounded kind of lame against that. Of course I wanted a family, kids, adoption or surrogacy, or whatever we could do. But between us, Jacob and I would make a permanent future, and if that was here in Minnesota, then I could go with that because there was no way I was spending years on the road with hockey to then be away from Jacob after that. I wondered if he knew how much I loved him and how long I saw us together and also whether he felt the same way. I knew he hated that we were apart, but he had his whole life on his family's farm ahead of him, and maybe he thought I wouldn't want that or that a coaching career wouldn't fit in with that.

"We could have some kids here, don't you think, Jacob," I began. "We could teach them to skate on the pond. I could coach them, and we can extend the house to add a wing or two. I just need a good contract offer, six years, maybe four mill or five a year, and we'd have the money to make a good life for a whole team of kids, actually probably more money than we need if we're careful."

Jacob's eyes widened, and he coughed, and I genuinely think I caught him off guard. "Extending the house, kids, coaching, okay, then." He pulled me close and hugged me tight, and I loved the way he held me, as if he was never going to let me go.

"I love you."

"I love you right back," he replied, and his expression was so intense and focused, and for a moment I thought he was going to say something profound, and then Scott snorted a laugh.

"I'm going to take up baseball and play for the Nats," he announced, and the ramped-up emotion in the room dissipated immediately. "But meanwhile, can we watch the freaking film?"

I wriggled back into Jacob's arms, and he leaned his chin on my head, and for a few moments, we watched the action on the screen, but I couldn't sit still.

"Sorry," I whispered and glanced up at him, catching his thoughtful expression.

"What for?"

"For mapping out our entire lives with kids and room extensions and money." Money was a sore subject between us, particularly because he wouldn't let me help pay for his dad's operation, but I'd learned that pride and Jacob were so closely entwined it was difficult to separate them.

"I liked you mapping things out," he said after a moment's pause where I imagined every kind of worst-case scenario. "You know that for me, what we have is forever, right?"

"Back at ya," I said and snuggled into him. "I could stay here all day with you. We wouldn't have to move at all."

"What about food?"

"Someone will feed us eventually, and we may even get beer as well."

"And the bathroom?"

He had a point. "We could have five minutes where we both use it and then come straight back to this chair."

"And showers?"

"You're overthinking this—"

"And the cows, you have to remember the cows." He was laughing now. I could hear it in his voice.

"We'd invent a machine that did everything for us, took care of the cows, moved the hay and whatnot, and did everything else you do."

He snorted a laugh then. "NHL star invents automated farmer, I can see the headlines now." He waved a hand in the air, imagining the title of the news report, and I struck a pose, trying to look completely serious, and when that didn't work, I stole Scott's glasses from his face and put them on.

"Do I look serious enough to invent a robot farmer?"

"Give them back, asshole," Scott interjected and flailed to get them off me, but Jacob held him off and kissed me soundly before finally handing them back.

Then he cradled my face in his hands.

"Do you think we can step outside?"

8

JACOB

THE MINNESOTA WINTER MET US AT THE DOOR. THE AIR was so cold it felt as if it could snap like peanut brittle. Ryker shuddered the moment his flesh—which had become accustomed to desert heat—felt the cold still air moving over it.

"I hope we're not going to be out here too long," he said, wrapping his arms around his middle.

"No, not too long." I stepped up beside him, draped my arm around his shoulder, and tugged him into my side. "Better?"

"Mm, yeah. You're like a big Bunsen burner." His curls rested on my shoulder as we gazed out at the pond, the soft glow of the moon making the thousands of skate slices show up in stark relief to the darkness of the frozen water below. I pulled my gaze from the pond and peeked at my man. Mom's lights glowed brightly, lighting Ryker's curls in shades of red, yellow, blue, and green. I buried my nose into his hair, just for a second, to get my thoughts in line.

I'd gone over this moment so often in my mind, but things had been different in my fantasies. Better. I'd had his ring for one thing. No one else had been around for another. The sounds of our friends now arguing over what to watch next, *Big Trouble in Little China* or *Remo Williams*, leached through the old door. Our future house was under construction in my fantasy proposal and the farm was thriving. Yeah, a fantasy for sure. Reality sucked.

"I loved the way we OU Eagles boys are making our families come to life. Sure they might be unconventional families, but they're families all the same," Ryker said as I sniffed his hair and daydreamed of the life I so wanted to give him. He lifted his head to peer at me.

"Yeah, families and futures. That's kind of what I wanted to talk to you about…"

"I'm sorry if I put you into a scenario that you didn't want to be in or even think about yet. Kids, dogs, that kind of thing."

There were so many things I wanted to say. None of them seemed adequate. "No, your dreams are perfect. Really." I released him slightly, just enough so that I could face him, my hands resting on his sweet, high ass, his fingers up by my ears. I looked down on him, his chin up, eyes sparkling, Mom's Christmas lights glowing on his face, and my words got jumbled up. "I've had dreams too. Every single one involved you. There's not a future scenario of my life that doesn't include you." He smiled softly, his fingers playing with the fine hairs on the back of my neck. "I had this all planned out, but life kind of tromped all over my carefully detailed designs."

"Dad says something about the best-laid plans of mice and men often going awry."

"Your dad quotes Robert Frost in one breath and Herb Brooks in the next. He's awesome."

"Yeah, he really kind of is." He rose up to kiss my stubbly chin. "So is this going anywhere, or are we just out here to see whose balls crinkle up in the cold first?"

That made me smile. *He* made me smile. And laugh. And cry. And love. Fuck, so much love.

"There's a purpose, just chill."

"If I got any more chill, I'd be a snowman."

"You'd be the cutest snowman ever." I dropped a kiss to his brow. "I just... there's so much I had planned out, you know me. I dislike not having things ready ahead of time. But things have gone... well, not right. And while I hoped this moment would be different, better for you, I guess I have to admit to myself that I might not ever be able to give you the best in life. I love you so much, Ryker, and I want you to be my husband, but I'm not sure that I'm the best choice for a spouse."

"Whoa, slow down, back up." His light brown eyes rounded. "Did you just ask me to marry you, then tell me that you're not good enough to marry me all in the same breath?"

"Yeah, well, no." His eyebrows beetled. "Okay, yes, mostly I was giving you an out. Nothing is going the way I planned, Ry. I'd hoped to have our home all laid out, maybe even the basement in before snow fell, but there was no money. I'd hoped to have a ring for you, and I did, but there was no money for the tractor, so I sold it. I'd hoped for so much for us, for you, but now there's nothing. There's nothing but my mother's ring, and that's not really suited for a dude. I've got nothing to offer you. Why are you even here with me?"

"Okay, first of all, stop it. Second, where's the ring?"

"In my wallet. I'm kind of embarrassed to—"

"Dude, *so* lame. You ask me to marry you, and you don't even show me my ring?"

"Ryker, it's my mother's ring. She took it off this morning and told me to give it to you. Your ring, the good one, the expensive one, I had to sell off to—"

He went to his toes, his lips covering mine. I stiffened at first but then slowly melted into the kiss, my hands roaming up and down his back as he licked into my mouth, his fingers tight to my skull.

"You're such a rockhead at times," he gently scolded when the kiss broke. "How many times do I have to tell you that all I need is you? Now, show me my damn ring, or I will throw your big ass out into the snow and take it."

I had nothing sensible to say, not a damn thing. I reached back, pulled out my wallet, and opened it gently, fishing the thin white gold band out with my pinkie. Ryker's eyes lit up as if he'd been handed the Hope diamond.

"Okay wow, that's so pretty with the Christmas lights shining on it." He slipped free of my arms and held up his left hand. It was shaking. "Put it on me."

"It's not going to fit." I felt foolish again, but he shook his head, curls bouncing, so strong was his head movement.

"Don't care if it fits or not. I want you to slide it onto

my ring finger as far as it will go. And I want you to look me in the eye and tell me that—"

"That I love you more than anything on this planet. That you're my life and love. That I hope I can make you happy and that I want to know if you'll marry me? Did that cover it all?"

"Yes. Ring, please." He wiggled his fingers. So I slipped the borrowed ring onto his ring finger. It went to the first knuckle. "I've dreamed of this moment forever." He looked up from his hand to me. "I would love to marry you."

I gathered him up for a kiss that went on and on and on and on. "I'll get you your own ring back, I swear." That was a promise I intended to keep, no matter what. I'd sell off my truck if I had to; didn't matter. Ryker's ring belonged on Ryker's finger. But for now, Mom's ring and Mom's lights seemed to have been enough to make it official. Ryker was mine now, and I was his, and the future seemed just a little brighter than it had this morning, so I kissed him again just because I loved him so damn much. We kept kissing until the guys rolled out onto the porch, yelling their congratulations as they hugged and slapped our backs. Okay, yeah, maybe life would all work out just as Ryker had dreamed it would. It *was* Christmas after all.

We were at the airport before dawn the next day saying good-bye to Ben, Ethan, Scott, and Hayne. There had been promises made to do this again, and then of course there were weddings to attend in the future. Ben and Ethan's was this summer, so we'd for sure meet up in

Canada for that if we couldn't find the time beforehand. We hugged and kissed cheeks and poked fun at each other.

Fingers meshed, Ryker and I stood inside and watched our friends take off. I glanced over at my fiancé, who was still half-asleep by the looks of it. A soft red ember of love and want unfurled inside me. He'd taken my mother's ring and placed it on the necklace he wore around his neck, something his baby sisters had given him last Christmas, with crossed hockey sticks. Seeing that ring lying against his skin moved me in ways I'd never imagined. I led him outside and to my truck, kissing him into a stupor before we rattled toward home. Mom had insisted we come for a big holiday breakfast today, even though the holiday was now over. Ryker napped on the way home, his head bobbing as I softly sang along to some Brooks & Dunn.

We'd no sooner pulled up when Mom appeared on the front porch, her hands clasped as we slid from the cab and made our way to her.

"Welcome to the family," she gushed, throwing her arms around Ryker. She sniffled a bit as she clung to him. Ry patted her back, grinning awkwardly at me. Finally, she released him and grabbed me for several kisses to each cheek. "We're both so thrilled for you boys. Come on inside. I made a big breakfast. Your father and I have a few things we'd like to discuss with you."

Taking Ryker's coat, I paused long enough to hang mine and his in the closet by the front door, then bent down to untie my Redwings. Ryker had kicked off his sneakers and was in the kitchen, shaking hands with my father when I showed up. Both men smiled at me. Dad limped over, gave me a brief hug, and then waved at the buffet my mother had made. Eggs, bacon, sausage, toast, coffee, and big homemade cinnamon buns for dessert. Breakfast dessert. Could be a new trend.

We sat down and dug in after Dad said a quick grace. When everyone had full plates and steaming mugs of freshly brewed coffee, my parents gave us both a look. It was the parent look. The one that said they had wisdom to impart. Given that we'd just gotten engaged, I assumed it would be sage wisdom about marriage, how it took two to make it work, how it was the little things that you argued about, how hard it was to keep a marriage thriving, that sort of thing.

I was buttering my toast when Dad cleared his throat. I glanced up from toast prep.

"We're selling the farm," Dad said. No preamble, no warming us up, no gentle introduction to his thoughts, just *BAM* right in the face.

"Dad, no, we're not selling." I sighed, having had this talk with them monthly over the past two years. "We can turn it around."

Mom spoke up, something she rarely did when we two men started butting heads. "Jacob, no, there is no turning it around. We can't make the mortgage payments and pay for your father's surgery. Also, we had a call last week from Roger Thompson with Agra-World and he put an offer in to us."

"You never told me that."

Mom and dad exchanged pointed looks, but it was Mom who gave the killing blow.

"We're meeting him tomorrow to start the paperwork."

My knife sort of slid from my fingers, hitting the table with a soft *thud*. I looked from Mom to my dad. He nodded. My gaze flew to Ryker, who was sitting beside me, mouth open slightly, his coffee cup frozen halfway to his lips.

"But…" I stammered, my thoughts all over the place. "But no, don't sell. Dad, Mom, we can do this. I just need to buckle down and—"

"We've buckled, Jacob. There's no way to tighten our belts anymore. Son, I am sorry, I know farming is your life, but I can't manage with this hip any longer," Dad confessed, and hearing him say that drove home the fact that this was really happening. "If we sell, I can get that new bionic hip. We'll have money for a small place in town, and you'll have the cash you need to pay off your student loans, buy back Ryker's engagement ring, and move out there to the desert to be with your *fiancé*."

My appetite, which had been so strong all morning as I'd done chores with Mom, faded. I placed my toast on my plate.

Mom gave me a reedy smile. "Honey, we know this is a shock, but is it, really? We've been struggling for years to turn a profit. There's just no money in farming anymore, and we're not getting any younger. If we sell now, we'll be set for retirement. And you can move on with your life. It's time, Jacob. You have Ryker now, and your life isn't here on this dying farm. It's in Arizona with your future husband."

"But I love this farm," I said, wincing when I heard

how childish I sounded. Yes, it had been my dream to farm this land as generations of my family had before me, but what about my folks? They had nothing now but crushing debts. If we sold, they could have a secure future with a nice nest egg for their golden years. What kind of son would I be to deny them a life free from pain and struggle?

"We know you do, son," Dad said.

I swallowed my emotion. "But, I love you too. I understand. I do. Ryker and I will be fine, won't we, babe?" I looked at him and he nodded in earnest.

Ryker nodded in silence. Mom reached across the table to take his hand and mine. Dad coughed. I suspected to cover what might be something emotional taking place.

"We know you will be. Now, we better get to eating before it all gets cold and I have to feed it to the chickens," Mom joked, but her eyes lacked humor. So we talked of other things while we ate, news and movies, hockey, inconsequential stuff. Light chitchat to help cover the fact that the Bensons were going to toss in the towel. A small part of my heart was breaking. Another family farm gone. A win for agribusiness. A loss for the small farmer.

We left my parents' house around noon for the cabin. Ryker had today to spend with me. Then I'd be taking him to the airport tomorrow for a ten a.m. flight that would wing him back west. We took the Polaris so that I didn't have to talk to him on the ride home. My stoicism was tolerated until we stepped into the cabin, which seemed quiet now that the guys weren't filling it.

"You want to talk?" Ryker asked, tossing his coat to the couch. I shook my head and slumped into the sofa, letting my head drop to the back. He sat beside me. I continued staring at the old barn boards on the ceiling. "You want to cuddle, then talk?"

"Yeah, please." I lifted my arm, and he shimmied under it. If anything could make me feel better, it would be Ryker.

9

RYKER

"I DON'T KNOW," JACOB SAID, WHICH WAS PRETTY MUCH ALL he'd been saying all day. This was Tucson apartment number six, and he'd found something wrong with all of them. The first was too small, second too big. I'm not even sure what was wrong with the third one, but Jacob was very quiet. Apartments four and five were too high up, and this was number six, which was on the fourth floor. It was neither too big nor too small, and was available in four weeks. The Realtor made it obvious that he was confused and quietly pissed, but I didn't blame him, poor guy. The spec we'd given him had been specific in only a few things. Two bedrooms were a given because I needed a room for all my gym crap. We wanted two bathrooms, one of which could be a half bath attached to the main room, and security downstairs.

The security had been Jacob's idea because he'd seen firsthand that even though hockey was still the least popular sport in this town, I was known. Part of that was due to Sebastian Brown's marketing initiative, putting

Alex front and center as the face of acceptance and diversity with a sexy spin and shoving me there next to him. The first time he'd seen the huge image of me on the billboard, right next to a poster for the new seasonal variety McDonald's Chicken Sandwich, his eyes bugged out of his head.

"Didn't you have clothes that day?" he asked when he saw the vast image of me and Alex, hockey sticks behind our heads, flexing every muscle we could. *Sex sells, darling, work that camera.*

"They made me take them off," I'd told him, and then when we were back in the apartment I shared with Alex and Henry, he'd been completely honest with me and told me that it was possibly the hottest poster he'd ever seen and could I get him a copy? He was teasing, and even now, I wasn't sure he was entirely happy with the whole moving to Arizona and having no farm thing. I'd been there the last day, when the Agri company had locked the gates, and we'd spent that morning at the old cabin, ice still thick on the edge, taking some photos to remember. He hadn't cried, although he'd held his mom when she had, and helped his choked-up dad into the truck to take them to their new home, a cute two-bed in town with a tiny garden and brand-new kitchen.

That had been two weeks ago, and he'd done what his parents had suggested and moved to Arizona to be with me. Right now, we were sharing my old room, but the plan was to get our own place, at the same time as he applied for all kinds of jobs in the local area. I'd never once said he could wait a while and that I would cover the rent and utilities because I knew my man, and he needed to work. Hard work defined him, and he'd searched through listed vacancies and had shortlisted a couple that were his preferred options, but he applied for everything that even vaguely mentioned agriculture, and I knew that with his degree and his life experience, he'd be like gold dust to anyone who interviewed him.

The one he wanted most, working at the U of A, had held interviews two days ago, and he hadn't heard yet, and I knew it was playing on his mind. He didn't have student loans to clear, but he wanted to make his fifty percent contribution to our new home, and I guess that was the real reason he was giving such vanilla responses to each place we looked at. He didn't hate any of them. He just didn't love any of them either, and as this was the last one today and my actual favorite, I needed to pin him down and talk. I held up a finger to the Realtor to indicate a time-out, and he nodded before backing away and out of the kitchen-dining-living area. Then I tugged Jacob to the window. From here, the view consisted of the park and more buildings, but if I craned my head, I could see the trauma facility that Henry was in, and the other way, the Raptors' arena. The commute was okay, the college wasn't far, we were close to the center of everything, and I wasn't sure what Jacob was searching for.

"I like this one," I said and tapped on the window. "See that park there? We can run there." He leaned his forehead on the window and peered down at Catalina Park.

"It's not a very big park," he murmured.

"Then we'll do laps." I forced all kinds of positive enthusiasm into my voice, and he glanced at me oddly.

"How much is it again?"

I pulled the sheet of paper from my pocket and made a show of reading it, even though I knew in great detail what it would take to rent this place. It was affordable on my income alone, not easily, but then we'd asked for two bedrooms. Give it another year, and if the Raptors held on to me and I got what Dad called my big boy's contract, then maybe we could buy outright, but for now affordability was a thing.

He was quiet as I listed not only the price but also the pros and cons of this particular property. Set in the older part of Tucson, it was solid brick and not a glass high-rise. It had gardens, and the security was good, so in my mind it was everything he said he wanted.

Only when he'd said that, he'd been positive about jobs, but everything was taking so long, and he was despondent and irritable about the delays, on top of the wrench of leaving the farm.

"Talk to me," I asked gently, and he turned his back to the view and sat his ass on the low window sill.

"The half that I need to cover, I only have enough for six months, and after that, if I don't have a job…"

I didn't sigh. I didn't immediately say that I would cover everything, because we were a partnership, and we shared everything fifty-fifty. Instead, I fingered the ring at my neck, clicking the joined hockey sticks through it, which had become my new lucky habit, and thought about the best way to approach this. Jacob's gaze fell to the ring, and he closed his eyes briefly.

"I don't know what to do," he said, and my heart ached for his confusion and worries. He'd left everything behind in Minnesota, and he had to start all over again to change his life plans.

"You'll get the job you want. I know you will," I encouraged and sat next to him, then elbowed him gently. He pushed me back and stayed leaning against me.

"You like this one?"

I cleared my throat, time for honesty. "Out of all of them today, yeah, I do. It's on a bus route, close to the U, there're two parking spaces, the rooms are big, and I've even thought about where we'd find a sofa big enough for us both. It feels homey, as if it's been waiting for us."

He nodded then. "One day, though, I want a house, with a yard, for the dogs and the kids."

"Same."

"But right now." He stopped and hunched a little, only relaxing when I took his hand. "Right now, I just need a job, money, so I can feel like I'm doing my part."

"I know."

I genuinely felt my fiancé was lost, and during the last few days, I didn't know what to do for the best. He sounded so miserable, and I'd noticed his introspective moments were lasting longer as time moved on after leaving the farm. I couldn't do anything about the job he'd interviewed for. I could only sit and wait with him, and hope everything worked out, and hug him when he was quiet, and be there for the low moments.

"How about this then. We tell the Realtor that we're not ready yet to make any kind of commitment financially, and we revisit this when I get back from the East coast road trip." Seven days apart was nothing for us. We'd done way worse, but now I had him here in my life, it seemed like a cruel and unusual punishment to be dragged away from him again. I love what I do, I'm freaking *good* at what I do, but it wasn't easy on any relationship.

"No," Jacob said firmly.

"No?"

"We have to take a chance on our future. Otherwise, we'll be stuck. This is my favorite today, and even if I end up flipping hamburgers, I will have a job by the end of this week. We can do this." He stood straight, and I saw focused, confident Jacob peer out through all the insecurities. "Let's do this."

I went toe to toe with him, cradled his face, looking deep into his eyes. "You're sure?"

He leaned in, and I slid my hands behind his neck and laced my fingers. "I'm sure."

So we called the Realtor back in, signed paperwork, and arranged to visit the office with deposits and every single piece of ID we had, and just like that, we had rented our own place. We walked back to the apartment I shared, slowly, taking in the city around us, holding hands and not giving a shit how long it took us to get back, even stopping to sit on a bench in Catalina Park, watching life go by. We were sitting quietly when his phone rang in his pocket, but I didn't think anything of it until he glanced at the screen and his eyes widened. He answered immediately, standing and blurting out a hello before clearing his throat and starting again.

"Jacob Benson speaking…"

I stood next to him, desperate to ask who it was. He'd interviewed for seven positions, including the coveted U of A job he wanted, and this could've been anything. It was possible that whoever was calling was giving Jacob bad news, and I couldn't make sense of what was being discussed from his side of the conversation.

"Yes... okay, I have those... equine... uh-huh, sorry, yes... thank you... I am, thank you. Monday... I will." Then he grinned as he spoke, and I didn't have to understand any of the words because whatever he was hearing was good news. I gave him a thumbs-up, and his beautiful eyes brightened with so much emotion I wanted to yank the phone out of his hand and kiss him senseless. I did a little jig on the spot, which a couple of passersby smiled at, and a few others watched before moving on, and listened to the rest of the one-sided conversation. "I'm so excited... yes... thank you so much for this opportunity. See you Monday."

He ended the call, and for a few moments, he stood in silence.

"Which one?" I prompted and jabbed him in the side. "Which one, freak?"

"I didn't get the U of A technician job I wanted," he began, and my chest tightened because fuck, that was the one he wanted.

"But you said... on the phone..."

"They said they see all this potential, that with my real-life experience, hell, Ryker... Jeez..."

"What? What!"

He blinked at me, clearly in shock. "U of A actually offered me the manager trainee role, the one that I didn't think I was experienced enough for. It's ten K extra. It starts on Monday. I said yes." He sounded as if he couldn't believe what he was saying, and then he picked me up and swung me around in the bright sunlight, and we whooped and hollered until we were hoarse.

I speculated how many of our future neighbors were looking out of their windows and wondering who the idiots were in the park.

I bet it was all of them.

EPILOGUE
JACOB

ARIZONA WAS WEIRD. WEIRD IN A GOOD WAY, OF COURSE.

I'd been living out here for over a month now, and I still couldn't get used to it being March and there being no snow. It was weird to wear shorts and sandals near Valentine's Day. Also, the cacti were peculiar. People had them in their yards as we Minnesotans had maple trees. I was just waiting to see a tire swing hung off one of those pokey, skyward arms. Also, what was up with the yards? Where was the grass? I mean, sure, some folks had grass, but lots had rocks. Rocks. In your yard. Back home, we tossed the rocks *out* of the yard so we could mow the grass. Here, they had landscaped yards full of rocks, sand, palm trees, and cacti of various shapes.

Then there were the animals. I kind of missed seeing moose sauntering down the road. Out here, they had things that snuck into your shoes at night that would kill you if you crammed your foot into your sneaker. That was wrong on multiple levels. Scorpions, spiders the size of dinner plates, Gila monsters, and African bees. We didn't have African bees in Minnesota. Back home, the animal that killed the most people were deer, and that was caused by them dashing in front of your car, not by hiding in your shoe. On occasion, a trapper would run up on a disgruntled wolverine, or a hunter would piss off a bull moose, but none of them hid in your Nikes. The whole death-waiting-for-you-in-your-shoes thing freaked me out.

Aside from the weather and the lethal critters, I liked Arizona. My job was fantastic. I got to work with some really cool people while learning about agriculture in this part of the country. We worked in conjunction with the university and were doing research on various aspects of farming, such as irrigation and crop water requirements, cotton production and propagation, soils and crop fertility, insect management, equine and bovine studies, and weed control.

I was on a good salary with benefits, would be eligible for paid vacations, and had a chance for rapid advancement. There was also the opportunity to return to school for my Masters, and then I'd be looking at higher-level management opportunities, but for now, I was happy working the land and coming home at night to Ryker. Not that he was there every night, but after spending so much time apart, a few days to a week of him being gone was nothing.

My days off were spent either in bed with Ryker, and those were my favorite kind of days off, or out with the guys on his team. He'd gotten close to quite a few of his teammates—Ryker was that kind of guy. The one all the girls wanted and all the guys wanted to be. The guys wanted him too because the man was gorgeous. Not to mention Colorado Penn, the goalie who was half-tender and half rock star. Talk about sexy. If I wasn't madly in love with Ryker, I'd have been drooling over Colorado. Oh, and the big Russian captain, Vladislav Novikov. He was older than most of our friends but seemed to be showing up more and more. Which was cool. The guy's dry wit was funny as hell.

When we had time, we hung out and sported as we were all jocks, aside from Alex's man, Seb. But the handsome Brit seemed content to sit in the shade, whittle at his work, take pictures of the Raptors' bare, glistening chests, and toss out *bon mots* about any number of things from life to shoelaces to the proper temperature for a bottle of red wine. It's fifty-five, according to Seb.

Today we were packing Henry's things for the moving company arriving tomorrow. The small band of close friends Ryker, and now I, had made were there aside from Henry of course. He was still in the rehab facility a few blocks away, but his release to a place that Adler Lockhart owned was imminent.

"I can't believe I'll have this whole place to myself," Alex lamented as we tossed Henry's clothes into a trash bag. "What the hell will I do with myself after I get home from games?"

"Oh, I don't know. Perhaps you could spend that time with your handsome beau," Seb said, plucking the sweatshirt Ry had whipped into the bag out and folding it neatly. Alex leaned across the bed to steal a kiss from his man. They were a cute couple. Well-suited, as they said in the old days. Pity they felt they could only be this demonstrative around close friends and family. I mean, I got it, but it was still a shame people had to hide who they were. On a purely greedy-ass level, I was thrilled not to have to hide what Ryker and I had. I ran my hand over the small envelope in my front pocket for the thousandth time and whispered a silent thank you to my mother yet again.

"I think this whole thing is most odd," Vlad chimed in, hoisting a box filled with books to one shoulder as if it were packed full of confetti. "Why is Henry moving into a new house? Why does he not go home to be with his family?"

"Well, there are issues with him and his family," Ryker explained, handing a balled-up shirt to Seb for proper folding. The Brit rolled his eyes but shook out the shirt and folded it neatly.

"I feel like Henry's valet," Seb muttered but refused to let us pack the fast way.

"Hmm," Vlad said, the big Russian staring at the nearly empty room. "In Russia, family holds the highest importance. Not just our parents and siblings, but the extended family as well. It's a concept that I've had trouble grasping about America."

"The house he's moving into is huge, but it's all on one floor and is owned by the Lockhart family, who have houses all over the world," Ryker explained to our captain. "Adler Lockhart is kind of like family to me; he's been with the Railers for years. Seems there's an old friendship between Henry's older brother and Adler, so he's opened up his Tucson mansion for Henry to use."

Vlad contemplated this, then nodded once. "I understand that bond. Still, I wonder why Henry refuses to let his mother nurse him. That would be the traditional thing to do." I enjoyed hearing Vlad speak. His accent was subtle, and his English quite good compared to Stan's, the only other Russian I knew well.

"It's not always easy with family. Traditions sometimes have to take a back seat to being true to oneself," Alex stated before switching from what was a touchy subject for him to talking about food. The food talk led to food consumption. After a massive takeout meal from two local places, one Mexican and one Korean, we all went our separate ways. Vlad home to his trendy condo looking over Tucson, and my man and I to our new place overlooking the park. Night had fallen on the city and when we got home, instead of flopping onto the couch to watch whatever was on the DVR, I led Ryker out onto our small but homey balcony.

"Come here. I want to show you something," I told Ryker, tugging him to the railing.

"But there's a new episode of *Impractical Jokers*," he whined and gazed at the TV set longingly.

"Sal, Q, Joe, and Murray can wait for like ten minutes," I countered, pulling him up to stand beside me. The city was stretched out before us, the park lit up, and the mountains standing majestically in the background. "We should do some serious camping in the mountains," I said while discreetly sliding my hand into my front pocket.

"Yeah, that would be cool. Are we done here

because…" He waved a hand at the apartment. I ignored his whining and held out today's mail. He blinked at the small blue envelope that now lay on his palm. "What's this? Did your mom send me more recipes?"

"Open it." I stepped closer, slipping my arms around him, my thumbs hooking casually in the belt loops of his baggy cargo shorts.

He cocked an eyebrow but ripped the padded envelope open and shook the contents into his free hand. It was a tiny square of cloth. I lifted it from his palm, unfolded it, and then held up his engagement ring. The ring I had bought and sold a few months ago. The ring that had been liquidated when the jewelers back home went out of business after Christmas. The ring my mother and I had desperately searched for before finally tracking it down last week at one of those large shopping mall jewelers. Yet another small business driven out by corporations. Shaking off what would be an eternal sadness in my soul, I let the joy on Ryker's face help wipe away the doldrums that thinking about selling our farm always brought.

"Is this *the* ring?" he asked, and I nodded. "Holy shit."

"Mom should be a private detective," I joked, reaching for his left hand. He giggled nervously as if I'd not done this before. I had, with the small white gold band next to his golden hockey sticks, but this time it felt… perfect and absolute. Right. Now everything felt right. "I've waited forever to see that ring on your finger. I couldn't wait a single day more."

The band slid down his finger perfectly. He smiled at me. I took his face between my hands and captured his mouth, kissing him with every ounce of devotion I had in me. He moaned softly into the moment, broke the kiss with a sigh, and eased us back inside, closing the sliding door on the past and all its pain and worries. From now on, we were focusing on the future. And what an amazing future it was going to be...

THE END

Valentine's
HEARTS

an OWATONNA Wedding Novella

RJ SCOTT &
V.L. LOCEY

Love Lane Books

1

JACOB

My eyes burned. And no amount of rubbing them was helping.

"… the same thing all the time? Maybe we should experiment sometime. Do some hot and sour soup or beef and broccoli." Ryker's voice broke my concentration. I sat up, scrubbed at my face with my fingertips, and focused on the proposal that'd fallen to me to type up. Why me? I was the newest guy.

"Yeah, we should," I called back to my fiancé who was dishing up our late lunch/early dinner in the kitchen behind me. Mind snapping back to work from Ryker, I stared at my laptop resting on my thighs and tried to pick up the threads of what was, in effect, a groveling letter from the U of A ag department to the company that'd been paying us to research and report on their seeds and would hopefully continue to do so. I began typing, blocking out everything and everyone in my space.

Furthermore, through our technology differentiator we have made great strides in understanding the microbial interactions *of the latest Bygenta BG Triple Grow which have allowed us to lower the cost of drying time by 0.07 per bushel. Combining that with the higher yield growth and moisture advantage we see a possible change in bushels/acres needed to recoup additional seed cost from $3.81 BU/A to $3.27 BU/A. Further testing on Bygenta BG Triple Grow should show significant gains for hybrid high yield corn seeds if combined with above ground technology to combat the Southwestern Corn Borer. Additional testing could save farmers millions of dollars a year in management costs and—*

The lid of my laptop snapped shut. "Hey," I snarled. Ryker lifted the Dell from my thighs, placed it onto the coffee table, and then took its place. "I was in the middle of something."

"I know, you're always in the 'middle of something,' even on the weekends. You worked on Christmas Day and yesterday—and they were our two days off together."

"I didn't," I lied.

"Don't think I didn't see you take your phone into the bedroom and then not come out for an hour."

"I was…" I had no excuse really, because I'd been checking on overnight reports, but that was the job, and I had a deadline that coincided with Christmas Day, and then more on the twenty-sixth. Then I recalled a fact that made his accusations seem wrong. "How do you know what I was doing? You were in a turkey coma on the big day."

"A turkey coma that would've been better snuggling with you on the sofa." He was making it sound as if he was joking, but there was an edge to his tone. Why didn't he get that I needed to put the hours in—the same as he'd done getting to be a pro hockey player? He'd done the hours, *still* did them, and now it was my turn. I had all that defense in my head, but he didn't give me a chance to talk. "Eat." He settled squarely on my lap, a huge bowl of chow mein in his hand. I huffed at the interruption just as my stomach grumbled. "See, you're hungry."

He held the green ceramic bowl out to me; his dancing hazel eyes alight. Sighing, I took the bowl as he plucked some chopsticks out of his back pocket. Cradling the bowl to my chest, Ryker wiggled his ass around a bit then gathered up some savory noodles, bok choy, and a fat mushroom and led them to my mouth. I opened and let him drop the food in. Then he gathered some for himself, and then for me, and so on. We sat chewing, staring at each other, the weight of him on my thighs pleasant and arousing. When his tongue danced over my lips I grunted and wished we didn't have our meal between us. He licked in when I opened my mouth, moaning. He tasted of soy sauce and ginger.

"Do we have time?" I asked breathlessly when the kiss ended. He opened his mouth to reply just as his phone alarm sounded. We both mumbled in disgust. "Guess not."

"Sorry, we have a game tonight." He dropped a dry kiss to my brow and jumped up, leaving the chow mein behind. "We'll pick this up when I get home, yeah?"

"Sure, yeah."

His smile brightened the room. "Excellent. Finish that up. You'll watch the game?"

"Of course. Go. You know how Coach gets when you're late."

He looked as if he wanted to say something more but

he just nodded then ran off to change. Within minutes he was in a suit, his shades on, earbuds dangling round his neck, and his hand on the doorknob. I was still on our tan couch holding the bowl of takeout.

"Are you sure you can't come to the game? Maybe we could go out afterward? Check out that restaurant that we were talking about having the reception at?" He stood waiting at the door.

"I have to get this proposal done or I'd go," I explained for the fourth time. He forced a smile and bobbed his head, soft curls falling over his sunglasses. "As for that restaurant, I thought we'd decided it was too expensive for the reception."

"No, *you* decided it was too expensive. But whatever. I have to go."

I let the jab roll off my back. There were few things Ryker and I argued about, but money always seemed to be a problem. He tended to spend without thought, and I held onto every penny. I knew it was because of our childhoods. He'd grown up with Jared Madsen as a father, a hockey superstar who could afford to give his only child —at the time—anything he desired, from hockey equipment and cars, to cash for college. Then there was my childhood on a struggling dairy farm, wearing the same chore coat and boots until my feet busted out of them because my parents couldn't afford new ones. A farm that my parents had ended up losing. The cost of this wedding was a constant source of contention.

"Ryker, don't get pissy. I'm just saying—"

He threw a hand into the air then left, the slamming door jarring me. I blew out a long breath then pushed to my feet, tossing the bowl of takeout to the end table. I padded to the window to watch him. He stalked out of our brick building, cut through the small flower and cactus garden, and headed toward the arena. We could see it from our window. Brow dropping to the warm glass, I stared down at him until he disappeared from view.

"When will you learn to just shut up?" I asked myself then lifted my head and stepped out onto our tiny balcony. There was room for one chair and a tomato plant out here. I knelt beside the plant and touched the dirt. Dry. Everything out here was always dry. Heaving a sigh, I stood, went to get some water in a glass and my laptop, and came back out to give Mr. Roma a drink. Then I sat beside it, legs stretched out in front of me and I watched the sky for the longest time, wishing I had handled the most recent tense moment with Ryker differently.

"I just have to chill out, let him do the wedding his way, and everything will be fine," I said to my tomato plant. "Just stop fighting him about costs. I mean, who cares if we blow every penny in our savings account? What's financial security compared to having four hundred guests and shrimp canapés? What the hell is a canapé anyway?"

Mr. Roma just sat there in his pot, soaking up the sun. Man, I wished we had a dog. I missed dogs. I'd grown up with *the best* farm dogs. There was nothing like a dog at your side. They listened much better than a tomato plant. But there were no pets allowed here. To be fair, a small apartment with two men who worked/travelled all the time was no place for a dog. For a dog, we'd need a house. For a house, we'd need a down payment. For a down payment, we'd need to stop planning an extravagant wedding and put the cash aside. And here we were back at money again.

"Ugh." My head dropped back to the brick wall. Mr. Roma was no help at all. "I bet an Early Girl tomato plant would have had better advice."

My phone buzzed against my ass. Hoping it was Ryker calling before he entered the dressing room to say he was sorry, I lifted an ass cheek and yanked the cell free of denim. I was monumentally disappointed to see that it was Adam Isaksson calling—my boss and lead on the Bygenta study. The millionaire tech giant was all about sustainability, and determined to change the world—I felt honored to be part of this new future at inception, and he valued my input on all levels.

"Hey, Adam," I said as I flipped open my laptop and found the document I'd been typing before the Ryker/chow mein interruption.

"I'm glad I caught you. Do you have that proposal for Bygenta done?"

I looked at the mostly blank screen. I had two paragraphs. Did that count as done? Doubtful. My gut began to churn.

"I'm working on it."

"Good! Finish it up then bring it to me and we'll polish it tomorrow. They're eager to see our results so far over in the main office. I've told them about the incredible work that this team, and you in particular, have been doing. I'm calling everyone to ensure all the data has been double and triple-checked. After we're done we can grab dinner somewhere and discuss your future with Bygenta Agrochemicals."

On some surface level, it was nice to have him speak so highly of me. I'd been working my ass off on this project, and Adam had been supportive of all the time and energy I'd put into my work. Unlike Ryker, who only bitched about my job. Still, if I went to his place to work tomorrow Ryker would come unhinged. I sensed that Ryker disliked Adam for some reason he wouldn't cop to.

"But tomorrow is Sunday. I have plans with Ryker to ride out to the ten bakeries he has on his wedding list and—"

"Jacob, I know it's the weekend, and I'm sorry for calling you in, but this is too big a chance for you to miss out on. If it's any consolation, I had to cancel a dinner date with my mother in Tempe. And you know how much I love spending Sundays with her."

Yeah. I did know. Adam Isaksson was close to his mother and spoke of her with great affection. I'd learned a lot about Adam over the past few months of this massive study. If I could just wrap this job up with a stellar report, Adam had promised to drop my name when he reported to the main Bygenta office in Switzerland. Maybe I'd get a higher position with more pay, then Ryker and I could stop fighting over cash all the time.

Now I felt doubly shitty. "Sorry. I know this sucks for all of us. I'll be there tomorrow."

"Thanks, Jacob. Tell Ryker I'm really sorry for ruining your plans."

"He'll understand." I lied a huge lie. Even Mr. Roma

knew it and was judging me in silence as only a tomato plant can. "See you tomorrow."

I cut the call and then let my phone slither down my chest to my leg, then onto the cement. Great. This would not go over well. We'd had Christmas and the twenty-sixth off together, but that had been caught up in Skype calls, and visits, and turkey, and tomorrow — the one day Ryker had off before a Canadian road trip — I get called into work to prepare for some asshole from the main office in some other country. Gazing at Tucson's arid mountain backdrop, I longed for Minnesota and the soft lows of cattle. It was seventy degrees in January. No way would I ever get used to the lack of seasons.

I missed snow and cold so much I could taste it. This city and this small apartment were chafing at me. I needed a big farmhouse, acres of corn and soy to tend to, cattle to milk, calves to bottle-feed and raise. I needed a dog.

"Nothing personal, Mr. Roma." I reached over to pat his green leaves. There was no wagging tail or lick of my hand. Blowing out a breath that puffed up my cheeks, I opened my laptop, rolled my head, winced at the cracking of my neck, and dove back into the world of dry data and ass-kissing. This whole Arizona experiment was *not* working out as I'd envisioned.

IT WAS MIDNIGHT WHEN RYKER GOT HOME.

I was waiting up with a sour stomach, a fake smile, and a tray of chicken tenders right out of the oven. He'd had a very bad game, monumentally bad, according to the play-by-play man, not that I saw all of it, because reports waited for no man.

"Hey," he said after tossing his jacket and tie to the back of the couch.

"Hey. Sorry about the loss. Boston is always tough," I said while sliding his tenders off the cookie sheet and onto a plate. He eyed the tenders suspiciously. "I knew you'd be down after a rough game so…" I waved at his favorite food then served him the plate. "Blue cheese or ranch?"

"Ranch. I really shouldn't be eating this kind of stuff," he whispered as he lifted a tender from the plate and broke it in two. "I'll be doing ten miles on the treadmill tomorrow."

"You're pretty dedicated to your diet. A treat every once in a while won't hurt."

He smiled then blew over the half a tender, sitting on the kitchen counter. I unscrewed the lid to the dressing then squeezed a big dollop onto the edge of his plate. He rewarded me with a smile—the most beautiful smile on the planet. I'd better cherish it because once I told him about tomorrow it would be gone.

"You always know how to make me feel good," he said. I had to look away. I'd never been good at deceit. "What?" When I worked up the courage to glance back, his brow was furrowed like a well-worked wheat field. "You might as well tell me."

"Don't get mad." As soon as I said it I knew it was stupid to say that. His sleek eyebrows dropped into a 'V'. "I can't go visit bakeries tomorrow because I have to go to work."

There was a harrowing span of like fifteen seconds where he said or did nothing. Then he flung the dish of chicken tenders to the counter.

"It's Sunday. You don't work on Sunday. We set this up five weeks ago because it was the only Sunday I was home and not playing."

"I'm sorry, I am! I just… Adam called and said we need to get this update into Bygenta and—"

"Fuck that project, fuck Bygenta, and fuck Adam! This is our wedding, Jacob! Do you even care about it at all?!" His gaze snapped with anger and pain.

"Of course I care!" I fired back, feeling like a lowlife bastard.

"Do you? Do you *really* care? I'm killing myself with the planning and playing hockey and all you do is shoot down and shit all over everything I propose. What the hell kind of wedding do you want? Do you just want to go stand in front of some JP?"

"Maybe! At least that would be sensible. We're supposed to be saving for a house, Ryker! And kids. How do we plan to make all of that happen when we toss every penny we have into this stupid wedding?"

"Nice, so it's 'stupid.' Good to know."

"I never said the wedding was stupid." Fuck, I *had* said that. Shit. This was spiraling out of control quickly. "I didn't mean the wedding is stupid. I *want* to marry you. I want us to have what my parents have and yours have. It's just all this pomp and circumstance is… well it's stupid. You've fallen into the trap."

"The trap." He said it so emotionlessly that I knew I

was deep in the shit. "What the hell are you talking about?"

"Yeah, a trap. The wedding industry has warped peoples' minds. My folks had a small wedding at home. The pastor came to my grandmother's house and married them, then they had their reception in a hay barn followed with a short camping trip by a nearby lake. Why can't we do that? Why do we have to have canapés and silk tablecloths and two entire hockey teams?"

"Wow, so *this* close to Valentine's Day you decide to finally be honest with me. That's fucking great, Jacob." He threw his hands into the air, hurt and ire rolling off him in waves that seared my flesh and heart. "Just so you know, I've always wanted a big wedding."

"I know, trust me. It's all you talk about," I snapped, and his eyes widened. "It is! Ever since I asked you to marry me, you've told me over and over about how you wanted to find a pretty girl, have a big wedding, spend a couple weeks in Europe, and then settle down to raise kids."

"I never specified it had to be a girl!" He was jacked now and so was I. "I mean shit, Jacob, you're a gay man! Aren't you the least bit into having the kind of wedding that straight couples have been able to enjoy forever?"

I rolled my eyes. His jaw tightened. "I don't care about all the bullshit that goes with marrying you. I just want to marry you. I want a house and a dog and kids."

"So do I!" he shouted and I winced. "And I want a wedding to be proud of. Not some hayseed hootenanny in some miserable barn."

Ouch. Shit, that hurt. "Right okay, well, maybe we

should just rethink this whole thing then since my dreams of a wedding are so below your standards!" Now *I* was yelling.

"Maybe we should!" He spun, grabbed his jacket from the back of the couch, and headed to the door. I gaped at him as he stalked out into the hall. "I'm going to Alex's."

He jerked the door shut. My hands were fisted in rage and so I did the one thing I could think of. I stuffed the chicken tenders down the sink, flipped on the garbage disposal, and ground them up. Then I fought back tears for a minute or two or ten.

2

RYKER

I DIDN'T GO TO ALEX'S PLACE. HE'D TAKEN A PUCK TO THE chest in an energetic defense strategy that had happened because I'd fucked up and left him open. His courageous dive had been doomed to failure, and he had to be hurting, and the last thing he needed was his idiot friend to visit. No doubt Seb was tending to Alex right now, and I wasn't about to go over and interrupt what would be a calm and peaceful wind down from the adrenalin of a spiky game with Boston.

A match-up we could have won if I'd kept my head in the game. If I hadn't been worrying about Jacob, and the wedding, and that asshole Adam, and about my place in the Raptors team and wondering where the fuck my career was going.

"Fucking Boston," I muttered and took the next left, fully intending to just keep driving, but instead ending up in the empty parking lot of a closed Target, engine off, doors locked, and not knowing which way was up. I was angry and ashamed and disappointed, and we'd lost the game, and I was tired, and somehow all of that had become one big ball of angst. I ended up shouting some real crap at Jacob, then stalked out like a freaking teenager fighting with a sibling.

I should text him. Call him. Go the fuck home.

But that wouldn't make things right. It wouldn't make the real deep understanding of my psyche right now any better. Because I had all the reasons why I was messing up in my head, and Gretzky-help-me but every single one of them still made sense, which meant I was so not over the adrenalin spike that had smacked into me. I was resentful and I couldn't push it away because this Sunday together was going to be everything, and I'd been looking forward to it for so long. One day with Jacob, talking about our wedding, reaffirming that we actually wanted to get married, and he had to work. Fuck's sake. I couldn't help but resent his boss—Adam was a taskmaster who expected results, driven to the point of insanity, and he was taking Jacob with him.

Burning, evil, mind-numbing jealousy coursed through me, the same as it always did whenever I thought about Adam, the sexy, and newly single millionaire environmentalist, with his grip on *my* fiancé. Why would he make Jacob work on the one day we'd planned things? Why couldn't Jacob say no?

This was the Raptors' first home game in so long and that meant all of Sunday to myself, and I'd had a clear picture of how that Sunday was going to go. Jacob and I would have a lazy breakfast, get excited about the day, then make love like we hadn't done even on Christmas-freaking-day, not that I was counting.

Sue me, I'm counting.

Every time I tried to start something, he would kiss me and tell me he loved me, and I sure as hell loved him, but then he would fall asleep, or tell me he had a deadline and would I mind if he came to bed later. Of course, I said I didn't mind, but I worried. He wore a perpetual frown, had smudges under his eyes, and there had been more than one night when I'd woken up and the bed was empty. He defended that what he was doing was worthwhile, and told me I was wrong to tell him he needed sleep, but that was starting to piss me off. Only the argument tonight hadn't been about sex, or sleeping, or any of those things; it was a childishly stupid lashing out, messed-up, and yet again I'd acted out of character, and I'd said some terrible things.

I could lose him. *What am I without Jacob? I'm nothing.* Just a hockey player with an attitude that stunk worse than the cowshed at his parents' old farm.

I wanted him to be here with me now, so I could stop feeling as if my entire world was about to end. What the hell did I even shout at him? Did I really feel that the wedding he wanted was below my standards? Had I really built up this amazing day in my head as a way to show off what I had, and did I really think that the two of us getting married in a barn was such a bad idea? Was it all about me and what I wanted? *What the hell is wrong with me?*

I banged my head on the steering wheel a couple of times and then rested my forehead there.

"Fucking idiot." My cell chimed with an alert, and I scrambled to get it out of my pocket. It had to be Jacob telling me to come home and that it was all okay, and we could talk. But it wasn't, it was Dad posting to our messaging group with yet another picture of Lottie, lit by a lamp in an otherwise dark room. The caption was a ton of emojis depicting the various stages of a night feed from the poop emoji to zzz's. I knew he and Ten were two hours ahead of us, meaning it was three a.m. in Harrisburg, and maybe I should call him if he was up? But, what would he tell me in his I'm-a-dad-and-I-know-things kind of way?

"You're an idiot, Ry!" I mimicked my dad's voice, which didn't take much, given we were so similar. I sent a text asking if he was awake enough to talk. He rang back and I smiled as I picked it up.

"Ryker? You okay?" It wasn't Dad, it was Ten, and he sounded sleepy but concerned.

"Shit, Ten, sorry, I thought my dad was up."

Ten yawned. "Nope, my turn, no game tomorrow, day off means I get to be up with Lottie, but we leave our phones out here." He yawned again, which made me yawn, and Ten chuckled. "Couldn't sleep after your Uncle Brady messed you up?"

"Ha freaking ha." Ten's older brother, and hence my uncle, was captain of the Boston Rebels and didn't go easy, even on his much younger kind-of-nephew. Of course he wouldn't, we were two grown men, and even though he was in the twilight of his career, he was one of the best in the league. Same as the other two Rowes, Ten and Jamie.

"You were doing some weird shit in that game tonight."

"How do you even know that?"

"We record your games and fast forward them to all your bits as soon as we come home. You need to… oh, I'm too tired to talk hockey, so if it isn't hockey you're calling about, wassup… s'okay little one, I'm here," he murmured, and I realized that last part wasn't for me as I heard the soft burbling of Lottie letting Ten know exactly what she wanted. My little sister had it so easy, bottle, poop, sleep, and all on her own schedule, no messy relationship stuff at all.

"Nothing, it's all good," I lied.

"You know you can talk to your step-dad, little Ryker."

"Go fuck yourself, Ten."

Ten chuckled, murmured to Lottie, and then sighed. "Are you and Jacob fighting again?"

"What? No. Of course not," I lied again. Why was I lying?

"Okay then, Lottie and I have an appointment with the sofa, you want me to keep you on hands-free so you can talk about whatever has you still awake?"

Did I? What could I say to Ten? Hell, I didn't even know what I would have said to Dad, let alone Ten, who wasn't that much older than me. What did Ten know about life and love and marriage?

Apart from being ridiculously happy with Dad, enjoying a glowing career with a team who only just missed the Stanley Cup, and caring for a new baby with the man he loves. No bigshot endlessly rich scientific innovator was going to come along and save the Earth was going to come along and steal Ten from my Dad. *Shit.*

"Nah, it's all good, say hi to Dad for me. Night, Ten."

How I kept my tone steady I didn't know, because that random thought about what might have been at the core of all of this took my breath. I'd known why I lost it so easily, and it wasn't about sex, or sleep, or not seeing Jacob—it was the specters in our lives. Adam and his job, and his demands on Jacob's time, and Tate on the team. And the wedding. And the pain in my hip from a bad check. None of my worries ever stopped.

"Night, Ry." Ten cut the call, and for the longest time I stared at the screen.

Someone banged on the car window, scaring the shit out of me, and I leapt up so fast I smacked my head on the interior. Adrenalin spiked, and I grabbed the keys to get out of here, then realized it was a cop. I turned on the power then lowered my window.

"Hi, Officer," I said, and I swear that there was guilt dripping off every single syllable.

"License and registration, sir?"

"Sure, absolutely, hang on." I retrieved both items slowly and carefully, light flashing briefly in my eyes, enough to make me blink and see stars.

"Not a good game for you guys tonight, Mr. Madsen," the cop said after a pause—all conversational as if he hadn't just scared the hell out of me and caused me to lose a year of my life.

"No, Boston was tough. We weren't," I admitted, falling into a familiar conversation.

"I have season tickets," the cop admitted, "bad luck last season."

"Yeah, we were close."

He handed back my documents. "You want to tell me what you're doing in a parking lot at one a.m.?"

"Thinking about the bad game," I lied.

He patted the roof. "The plate was called in by three separate concerned citizens, and you're on CCTV, so you might want to do your thinking back at home. Let's move this along, okay?"

"Yes, sir, Officer, of course." I started the engine and had my finger nearly to the window control when he tapped my roof.

"Also, tonight's game? The buck stops with you, Madsen, stop hogging the puck," he suggested and then sauntered away.

I felt like a kid whose peewee coach was telling me to play fair. I was used to fans critiquing my game, and sometimes they were right. *He was right.* I had so much to prove, to Brady, to the Boston team as a whole, to Coach who told me my head wasn't in the game, to Jacob proving I was a better man than Adam. To Tate, who probably saw me as second fiddle. Shit, I was a mess. Then I'd frozen out Alex, leading him to dive in front of the puck. His bruised ribs were all on me. Then I'd taken that whole shit fest home even though I promised myself I wouldn't, and all it had taken was for Jacob to mention Adam and that was it, I spiraled like a stupid ass kid with no filter.

"And I want a wedding to be proud of. Not some hayseed hootenanny in some miserable barn?"

I groaned at my stupidity. Who even says something like to that to their fiancé, when the whole reason I'd fallen in love with him was because he was so grounded?

He was my touchstone, the person who kept me tethered so I didn't do stupid things like lose my shit over one crappy game.

But what if I'd fucked up too much this time and he didn't need me anymore? What if *Adam* was showing him a good time in among the seed reports and the business meetings? What if the gorgeous, rich innovator was making moves on Jacob? Was a wedding to impress everyone else what we should've been aiming for? Why was I even doing this?

I drove home in a fog, thankful that every light went my way, and that I didn't get pulled over for cruising the neighborhood in my aimless fashion, until finally I was back at the apartments and turned the engine off. My highly impractical sleek black car looked so wrong next to Jacob's truck, and I'd never seen anything sadder than those two next to each other. I was flash and money and selfish jealousy, he was solid and stable and working so hard for what he wanted. I knew I worked hard as well, but he had so much on his plate, all the projects and the late night calls and the impossible deadlines.

All I'd done was lose a fucking game, and I was part of the problem in the team.

Jacob loved me, I knew he did, and every couple had arguments; hell, I was sure Dad and Ten argued about things, although I'd never seen it myself. Pulling out my cell, I sent a quick message to Alex, apologizing for the situation I'd put him in, another to Coach explaining I needed to talk to him about the Boston game and pre-empting him calling me into the office, then a final one to Vlad with an apology for being an ass. The only one who replied was Coach, who suggested I wait until Monday and that we all had bad games, and that I needed to leave whatever was messing with my head outside the arena. I didn't reply with a quip about why he was up so late, because we'd lost, and he was probably restless with questions about what had gone wrong.

Aren't we all.

Then, there was nothing for it, I had to go up and face Jacob, apologize for being an idiot and not accuse him of something shit, like choosing Adam over me. The devil in my head whispered that Jacob had said some awful things as well, and that he had blown off our one special day together, but the angel in my heart shoved that little red asshole aside. By the time I made it to our apartment I was fried, physically and emotionally, but I needed to climb into bed with Jacob, wake him up, hold him tight, and promise him the world all over again.

"You came back," Jacob said from the darkness of our living room, then switched on the small lamp that Colorado had bought us when we moved in. It was a patterned orange and purple, the colors of the desert, according to him, and I swear there was the shape of an emu in the swirls, but I couldn't be sure. The lights on our small Christmas tree cast a colorful glow in the other corner, and a silver star on the top caught the light and threw it over Jacob's features.

"Of course I did."

"Where did you go?"

"Around. I actually ended up sitting in the parking lot outside Target and almost got arrested."

"What?" Jacob stood then, buzzing with righteous

indignation. "You can't be arrested for sitting in a parking lot."

I stepped into the glow cast by the lamp. "I think the cop actually would have arrested me for fucking up tonight's game."

"You didn't," Jacob defended immediately.

"I did. I was all over the place, selfish with the puck, too much in my head I think, worrying about the game, the team, Adam, you."

True to form he picked up on the one word that I'd slipped in which was the bone of contention in our home. "You have nothing to worry about with Adam."

"Nothing to worry about from the sexy millionaire with the mansions and the cars, and did I mention the sexiness and the way he's always touching your arm, and smiling at you?"

Jacob worried at his lip, and I could see his thoughts jumping from one scenario to another, but before we started to argue again about a ghost who shouldn't even have been in the room with us, I stepped into his space.

"I'm sorry," I began.

"Me too. He's like that with everyone, demanding, and this job means too much and with Adam I—"

I didn't want him to mention Adam, so I talked right over him. "I'd get married naked in the desert with Colorado's grandmother officiating, and with an emu as the best man, if it meant I had you in my life forever." I'd framed the admission as a joke to make Jacob smile, and he tugged me into his arms and held me tight. I didn't *really* want to stand naked in front of Alchemy and an emu, or indeed Colorado, but truth be told I'd go anywhere and do anything just to marry Jacob.

"About the cake. I choose chocolate," Jacob murmured. "Any kind of chocolate cake, but I've been thinking that maybe we take up Apollo's offer to make it, instead of going to some impersonal cake place we don't know…? He could come here before the New Year, and I'm sure we can fit in talking to him about what we want. Together."

"Next thing, you'll want me to talk to Alchemy about officiating," I joked again, which was apparently one quip too far. Jacob stepped back a little and cradled my face.

"The wedding will be wonderful however it happens, and I can't wait to marry you, but I want it to mean…" he paused and rested his forehead to mine.

"What?"

"More. I want it to mean *more*. I don't want to be on show, I don't want to make a huge flashy statement about marriage equality, I want to marry the man I love, and I get you're a public figure but… please let this be about us."

I bristled a little, but that was to be expected, because the core of everything—marrying Jacob—was important, but in my eyes the other things were as well. Proving to the world I loved Jacob, and that I was entitled to love him, and that we were happy, was vital to me.

But was it because I wanted to show the world? Or was it to show Adam?

"Let's go to bed." Jacob flicked off the lamp, and we headed to our room, falling into bed and holding each other tight. We didn't make love, or talk; we wrapped our arms around each other and slept.

I'll deal with the rest in the morning.

3

JACOB

THERE'RE TONS OF THINGS THAT I COULD'VE GROWN TIRED of. Old songs, out-of-style clothing, cartoons that were hilarious when I was six but were not so funny now that I was an adult, things such as bias, hatred, the usual crap.

But, one thing I'd never tire of was waking up next to Ryker and watching the sun dance across his curls. He tended to sleep on his stomach, long legs tangled in the bedding. This morning, his arms were over his head and his strong back bare. I rolled to my side, eager to touch. His hair was satiny smooth. I ran my fingers through the thick mass, enjoying how it would bounce back after each stroke.

"Mmm," he sighed into his pillow. I dropped a kiss to his arm. "Mmm again." I nipped at his shoulder. "Mmm times three."

"I want you," I murmured, peppering his back with love bites as I ground my hard dick into his hip.

"Want you too," he replied, lifting his sweet ass into the air. I licked my way down his spine as I slid over him.

Chest to back, I aligned my cock with the crack of his ass. His fingers tightened on the headboard. "Lube, now."

He didn't have to repeat himself. I grabbed the pump bottle from the nightstand, coated my cock, and pressed him down into the bed. I still had a few inches and about thirty pounds on him. Not that he was a pushover. The man was a powerhouse, but in bed, he was malleable and eager to be taken. I straddled his thighs, my slick fingers spreading his cheeks then toying with his hole.

"Come on, baby," he huffed, his plea more than enough encouragement. Easing into him was glorious.

"God you're hot," I groaned as I slid in deeper, my fingers biting into his buttocks. Watching my dick disappear between his round cheeks made me mad with want. I thrust hard, burying myself inside him. Ryker tossed his head back, curls falling over his neck. "Ready?"

"Yeah, shit, fuck me. Hard. I want to feel you all day," he growled as he gripped the edge of the mattress.

Being a courteous lover, I gave my man what he desired. With the desert sun beating in on us, I pumped like a wild man. He locked his arms over his head, gripping the headboard, his back now coated with a sheen of sweat. It had been a week since we'd last had sex so our orgasms rode us with speed. He came first, blowing his wad all over the bedding, his body clamping on my dick. Lost in the sensation, I grunted and heaved myself down and over him, grabbing a meaty thigh and hoisting it up and to the side.

"Fuck, fuck!" Ryker shouted as I nailed his gland over and over. Watching him under me, writhing and humping the bed, I lost the tiny bit of control I'd had. I dropped onto his slick back and came inside him, shuddering with each pulse.

"Ry, baby, shit," I whimpered, holding on then throwing my weight to the left. My cock slid out then, coating his ass cheek with spunk. He softened in my arms. I sucked on his throat as I searched for his cock. I took his dick in hand. He pumped into my fist a few times before he melted in my embrace. "Love you, love you so much," I whispered beside his ear before taking the lobe between my teeth.

"Love you... so much," he replied breathlessly.

We lay there working to catch our breath, our bodies cooling, content with the world.

"We got a mess," Ryker stated the obvious.

"I know." I sighed, kissed his cheek, my lips enjoying his new whiskers. I cinched him closer. "Sorry for... well, everything. This job—"

"Nope, don't go there. Let's just enjoy us, this, for a little longer."

So we did. Just for a little longer. Then we had to peel ourselves away from each other and face the day. Showers, skip the razors, clean bedding, a quick breakfast of eggs and honey ham slices with coffee, and then the call to Apollo was made.

I could hear Henry's boyfriend squeal with joy after Ryker asked if he would help with the cake. Guess Apollo thought cake meant wedding, because in less than an hour he was at our house, seated at our kitchen island looking at wedding magazines with us, Henry, and Apollo's aunt Maria. I imagined we'd have time to think about this, but nope, here he was, and I still had stuff to write on the report, and I could see my laptop from here.

"I am so excited for this!" Apollo beamed as he tossed about twenty wedding magazines to the countertop. "I know you've been having troubles deciding, so now all the troubles will be mine! I'll be the best wedding planner ever!" I glanced at Ryker. He was agog, his lower lip between his teeth. "First, we need to pick the perfect place. I know where that is! Not too big, not too fancy, and price wise it will be perfect!"

"We're not getting married at Adler's mansion," I quickly interjected because Ryker was obviously having speech issues.

Apollo frowned for a moment then snapped his fingers, setting his bangles to jingling. "No, stop, I was not suggesting the halfway house. There are too many patients there now. A wedding might be too much stimulus for some of them." He tapped his phone. "I was thinking of using Colorado's desert camp. It's remote but beautiful. And cheap!"

"Uhm…" I said and nudged Ryker. He blinked. Great. "Uhm, well, I'm not sure Colorado would—"

"Of course he would! Look, I'll call him!" He swept around the room with his phone to his ear. Henry sat beside me smiling softly as his man took over.

"Colorado, hello, it's Apollo. I'm putting you on speaker."

"Dude, what's up?" Colorado's raspy voice filled the kitchen.

Apollo held the phone out. "I'm here with Ryker and

Jacob, the soon-to-be newlyweds, they've turned to me to plan the wedding-slash-reception," Apollo winked at me.

"Cool! Your parties are epic. Almost as killer as mine."

Maria crossed her long legs and sipped her coffee.

"Well your party days are over and so it falls to me. Since I have an easy schedule at school I'm happy to help these two. They're here. Say hello boys!"

"Hey," Ryker and I said in tandem.

"Yo, guys. Man, tying the knot is huge. How can I help?"

"They want to use your camp out in the desert," Apollo quickly replied.

"Oh sure, go for it. Do with it what you will. Oh, hey, got to roll. Joe and Maddy Boo are ready for a trip to see Kricker. The camp is yours! Later!"

The line went dead.

"There! Done! The wedding will be at the camp as will the reception. I'll do the food because, in all honesty, I am one hell of a cook!" Apollo beamed.

"He is," Henry agreed and got a buss on the cheek from his man.

"Such a sweetie! So, wedding food is taken care of. Auntie here will do makeup and hair!" Apollo patted his aunt's arm.

"Guys don't wear—" I started to say then Ryker drove his elbow into my ribs. Apollo's big brown and lined eyes locked on me. "I mean… Ryker and I don't wear makeup."

"I can do your hair then," Aunt Maria said then took a sip of coffee. "Although you could use some concealer maybe, and some powder, just for the photographs."

"Uhm…" I said again then was steamrolled by Apollo

tossing out menus while his aunt held up color palettes next to our faces while babbling about moisturizers and anti-shine powders and subtle applications of a gel comb on our eyebrows. It was noon before they left, Apollo and Maria chatting away, Henry shaking our hands at the door as he juggled the magazines.

"I know they seem overwhelming, but trust me, they'll do a great job for you guys," Henry said. We both nodded. He smiled at us then jogged off.

I closed the door and looked at Ryker. "Well that certainly went differently than I expected," I said.

"Yeah, me too. Did we even mention chocolate cake?"

"No, not once." I chuckled then pulled him into a warm hug. Burying my nose in his hair, I inhaled. "I don't really even care about cake flavors. I just want to marry you and start our lives together. Are you okay with the camp? I know it's not a fancy church followed by a massive reception hall."

"Actually, the camp is fine. There's plenty of land for the teams to explore, no neighbors to worry over sound issues with, and I bet it's plenty romantic at night." He nuzzled my chin with his nose. I kissed him, hard, and with so much yearning it hurt. "I just want you to be happy."

"Same baby." I stared into his beautiful hazel eyes framed with thick dark lashes. "I think we may have compromised."

His smile made me weak in the knees. "I think we did. And all we had to do was turn over the biggest day of our life to Apollo Vasquez, party master extraordinaire."

I loved seeing him happy. "Want to go back to bed?"

My phone rang then, and I knew exactly who it would be. As did Ryker. The playful aura surrounding us dissipated.

"I better get that." I left his arms to grab my phone before it hit the floor.

"Yeah, best jump for him," I heard Ryker mumble as I swept the phone off the counter. The muffled jab hit dead center but I didn't respond. Instead, I replied to the text Adam had sent reminding me that we had a lunch date. I stared at the word *date* for a second, feeling funny about it for some reason. Shaking that off, I hit him back to tell him I was on the way in five.

"It's Adam," I said after sending off my text. Ryker nodded. "This won't take more than a couple of hours. Do you want to come along?"

"No, I…" He shook his head. "No. I don't. I'm going to go work out, maybe call Alex to see how he's doing, get caught up on that Lovecraft show."

He was stiff now. His words clipped. Fucking work. This was so not how I'd envisioned my job being. Maybe I needed to tell that to Adam. See if I could back out of the Bygenta program and find something less tech-based and more animal-based.

"Okay, well, I'm going to grab my laptop and go."

He nodded.

I rushed to grab my Dell then change into clean jeans and my old Owatonna T-shirt. Ryker was spread out on the sofa when I emerged from the bedroom. I bent over the back of the couch for a kiss. He puckered. The touch of our lips was brief.

"Right then," I said as I straightened up. "Glad we got

the wedding stuff figured out. I think it will be amazing, Ry."

"Yep, me too. Amazing." His attention was on the TV.

Exhaling softly, I grabbed my wallet, keys, sunglasses, and laptop then backed out of the apartment.

My truck was hot, because even in freaking winter it was on the warm side in Arizona, and so I eased into Sunday traffic, my mind looping over a thousand things as Blake Shelton sang a sad song about a love lost. I never wanted to lose Ryker or what we had, but I was beginning to suspect that somehow, somewhere, something was going to have to change. I could see he wasn't happy. And that saddened me. All I wanted out of life was to make Ryker happy. And I was failing at that.

By the time I reached Rattlesnake Peak Road, I'd fallen into a funk. I rolled to the gates of Adam's land and rang the buzzer. They opened slowly. Pulling up to the nine thousand square-foot Spanish motif mansion didn't help to lift my spirits as it should have. Adam whipped open the wide front doors and stepped out to greet me. That made me smile. He was a nice guy. Smart, professional, outgoing, eager to help those under him succeed. Add to that, he was easy on the eyes, dressed impeccably, and came from a ranching background, and it was easy to see why every woman and most of the men on the project respected him. For some crazy reason he had picked me, the big, bumbling farm kid from Minnesota, to take under his wing.

"Good thing I told the cook to put the food in the oven on low," he said as I exited my truck. He took my hand, shook it, and then held it for a long moment. The sun seemed to glint off his gold hair as his sky-blue eyes twinkled. He had some age lines; he *was* over forty, but they suited him well. Lean and tall, not as tall as me though, he commanded respect with his bearing. He'd come far from his humble roots on a dirt-poor horse farm in Wyoming.

"Sorry, the cake discussion kind of went off the rails and we somehow ended up with a wedding planner and makeup artist," I replied then eased my hand from his grip. He did tend to be a little too much in my personal space with the touching, but I chalked that up to Adam being Adam. I could handle a long handshake or an arm around the shoulder as long as it was brief.

"Ah weddings. I hope yours runs smoother than my first two did. My last husband cost me a Malibu beach house and several Arabian mares."

"Ouch, sorry."

He patted my cheek playfully. "Don't let me drag you down. God knows the older a man gets the less trust he puts in vows and promises. Much better to just stay single." He looped an arm around my shoulder then led me past the infinity pool. "I told Marta to set up our food on the veranda overlooking the guest house."

"Do you have power there for the laptop? My Dell isn't holding a charge."

"Of course, but also I'll send you a new laptop."

"It's okay I don't need—"

"Nonsense, I can't have my best analyst working on old equipment."

That conversation over, we strolled around the grounds, him talking about the weather and the new groundskeeper he had hired, small talk for a millionaire. My eyes swept over the vista, the desert hills, and tall cacti as I grew more and more uncomfortable with his arm around my neck and managed to shuck it off jokingly. Thankfully, we reached the back of the mansion. A huge in-ground pool sparkled under the afternoon sun.

"Did you bring trunks?" he asked, his hand sliding down my back to rest on my belt as he directed me to a small round patio table heaped with covered dishes. I sat facing the wind feeling more than a little uneasy. He took my laptop, placed it onto a matching glider to the left of us, and poured me a drink.

"No, no trunks."

"Never mind, next time maybe." Adam looked the part of wealthy homeowner in his khaki shorts and tailored blue button-down. "I had Marta prepare some of your home state favorites." He pulled the lids off the platters. My eyes widened. "Walleye fillets over wild rice, venison meatballs, a pot of booyah soup, and of course, some cold Grain Belt beer to wash it all down with."

I eyed the ice-filled urn holding several bottles of beer. "I'm not drinking."

"I'll have my driver take you back."

"No, I'm good. I need to concentrate on the figures anyway. And, oh man, the only thing that's missing is a tater tot hotdish," I laughed.

"Damn it! Next time." He ladled up some of the rich soup and passed the bowl over. I dug in, sighing at the taste that took me right back home to fall church fundraisers where the booyah was made in huge kettles to sell. It was just as good as I recalled. The meats—oxtail, pork, short ribs, and chicken were tender, the veggies soft and delicious. I spooned up a big chunk of rutabaga. "Is it a taste of home?"

"Oh yeah, it's just like the church socials back in Minnesota. I really miss the cold weather." I sighed then resumed eating.

"I bet. I miss the snow. Growing up in Wyoming, I always loved the arrival of winter when I was a kid. Which is why I enjoy spending as much time in Switzerland as possible. It's the home base of Bygenta, and winter there is really winter! You know." He cracked open a Grain Belt and passed me a lemonade. "This project is nearing completion. Once it's done I'd love to fly you over to our HQ in Basel. Do you ski?"

I nodded then dabbed my chin with a heavy cloth napkin. "Yeah, of course."

"You'd love it over there then. They have some wonderful snow already, and the ski resorts are to die for! I own a small chalet near Basel-Landschaft with access to some amazing slopes. We could ski all day and enjoy the town of Basel at night. They have a winter market that I hit weekly, some wonderful ice-skating rinks, and the food is simply incredible!"

"Sounds great." And it did.

I doubted Ryker would think so though...

4

RYKER

THE MEETING WITH COACH CARMICHAEL ABOUT THE Boston game went much as I'd expected. He'd been controlled but pissed, I'd been irritable and defensive. When he suggested I explain what in heaven's name I'd been thinking to take my eye off the puck, I told him I had my reasons. He contemplated me over his steepled hands for some time and then sighed.

"Do you actually want to play Raptors hockey?"

What the hell kind of question was that?

"Of course, I do!" He frowned at me. "Coach," I added with respect.

"It doesn't seem like it right now."

"It's just..." I folded faster than Superman on laundry day, and poor, bewildered Coach Carmichael got the full story of my life as it stood, with all the resulting hesitations and worries. Well, the edited version, at least. When I was done with my fabricated excuses, he sat back in his chair and regarded me thoughtfully.

"So tell me what you are doing to fix the hockey parts?"

I could answer that one in my sleep. "I'm going to put one hundred and ten percent into every game."

"And?" He leaned forward and tapped his pen on a pad of Raptors notepaper filled with Xs and Os.

And? He wanted more from me? Like what? "I apologized to Alex," I offered, and he raised a single eyebrow, which appeared was going to be his only comment. "And the team," I tagged on. He didn't have to know it was in group chat, but the post was sincere and heartfelt and talked about moving on to the next game. He remained underwhelmed and I wracked my brains for what else he might need. "I'll leave the attitude at the door when we play?" Shit, I made that sound like a question, and he didn't appear to be amused.

"Ryker, this isn't the first time in the last few weeks that you've been off your game, in fact the Boston mess was the fifth one in a row. So, I've talked to Charlie and he's waiting for you in his office."

I winced. Charlie Brewer, the team numbskull-whisperer, was the very last person I wanted to talk to. He was a nice enough guy, but he had this way of looking at a person as if he could see straight inside their soul. He wasn't a trained psychologist, but he was a former player and he knew his stuff, and was the one who stayed around to knock sense into anyone who needed it.

"That's okay, I'm good."

"It's not a request, it's a prerequisite to coming east with us. I don't want to make you a healthy scratch but

I'm not sure you and Tate are working your lines in the best way."

What? Benching me? And where did Tate Collins, wunderkind and all around nice guy come into this? I hadn't noticed any issues with Tate's line. In fact, Tate had been the one carrying the team over the last few games with the once famous JAR line imploding under my lack of playing the right way. He stared at me, and I met his steady gaze as realization slid through me and hot shame followed. He wasn't telling me that Tate and I had problems with our respective lines, he was suggesting that *I* had a problem, and that it was falling to Tate to fill the gaps, and that this was an issue. I deflated and slid down in my chair. Of course it was an issue.

"I'll see Charlie," I offered, a lot less confident than I had been before. I'd been relying on good old hockey bullishness to get me through this, but not only was I fucking up my relationship, I was fucking up the team.

"You can go now. He's waiting."

"I will." I almost made it out of the door when Coach called my name.

"Madsen? For what it's worth you have the capacity to be the best second line center in the NHL. The JAR line is your ticket to being not just ordinary, but great, so mend what's breaking before it's too late. And please, do it before management entertains one of the many offers they have for you in trade."

"They want to trade me?" I ran out of words in shock.

"No, fuck's sake, Madsen, go see Charlie, get your head straight, and I want your A-game when we head for the east coast road trip on January second."

East coast meant matching up against Boston again, playing Brooklyn, the Railers, Philly, New York, five teams where I needed that A-game. Coach was right, Jacob was right, Ten was right, hell, the cop outside the store had been right. I was shit at the moment and I needed to be better.

I grumped and sighed my way up to the top floor where management had offices, along with Charlie in his pastel-toned room with its soft chairs, privacy blinds, and cushions, and knocked on the door.

"Ryker, come in." What Charlie didn't know about hockey wasn't worth knowing, and his brain held years of experience and understanding. I'd heard on the player grapevine, likely from Vlad, who was the font of all knowledge, that Charlie was supposed to have retired a few years ago. He was a Hall of Famer player from the seventies, then a scout for Vancouver, but I guessed the intrigue of working for a failing team like the Raptors was enough to extend his career. Now he was in a plush corner office with a neat desk, glass walls, and a gorgeous view of the city, dispensing advice to idiots like me. So far I'd avoided ever needing to see him, because I had a happy home life, no money worries, no exes causing trouble, my family was solid as well... But now... I was supposed to be on top of the world, getting married, facing down teams and getting goals and... I wasn't.

"Ryker, hey. Shut the door."

I did what I was told and then he waved me to the nearest seat and pressed a button to shut the blinds. I had a moment of panic as the room isolated itself from the outside world, and then I slid on the soft leather and got a throw cushion stuck under my ass for my troubles. I ended up sitting crooked for as long as it took me to fish the evil purple thing out from under me and toss it to the next chair.

"Coach sent me," I blurted when Charlie looked over his glasses, wearing a benign smile. I imagined he'd launch right into what I was doing wrong, but instead he smiled at me.

"Did you know I was lucky enough to play against your grandpa? Scrappy, hard to defend against, kinda evil in the corners."

"Cool." I should have put two and two together—of course, Charlie and my grandfather would have connected through seventies hockey in the age of glam rock and flares.

"Then I scouted your dad, shame Vancouver didn't manage to grab him."

What was this? Family history time? "Uh huh," I offered cautiously, and he bobbed his head.

"So, are you injured? Or is it the fact that Tate coming has pushed the JAR line to second, or is it a weird-ass thing you have going on completely unrelated to hockey?"

Talk about a quick change in subject. "I'm not injured, and I have no issues about being second line with the guys."

"Do you think maybe Alex has an issue? Maybe with you?"

"What?" This was news to me. Alex and I were close, and he would have told me if I was fucking him off, right? Hurt ripped through me that Alex wouldn't have just said something to me yet somehow Charlie sounded as if he and Alex had talked and—

"Ryker, I can see your brain overworking—I don't actually *know* what Alex thinks."

Relief flooded me. I knew he wouldn't do that without talking to me first because best friends confronted their issues.

Like I'm not *doing with Jacob? He's my best friend, but I'm holding back from him. I should tell Jacob that I'm an ass and that I love him even if I can't face up to my insecurities and jealousy.*

Charlie huffed. "Look, Madsen, I don't do all that fancy chat where I ask you about trauma or whether or not you're worried about the finale of some reality show you're watching, or whether a pet has died, I go straight to the core and I don't mess about."

"Okay—"

"Look at it this way. Tate Collins has come in to *your* team, taken first line, he's an acknowledged phenom, one of the best of his generation, blah blah, and you'd fought so hard to get the Raptors up to scratch and then they reward you by pushing you and your line mates down, and leaving you on the outs. Right?"

That wasn't entirely fair. I'd always known the minute Tate arrived that my shiny halo of being the shit was going to slip. All I wanted was what was best for the team.

What? Even if the best is Tate apple-pie Collins with his all-American smile and his perfect hair and his... well shit. Maybe I do I have an issue with him.

"I don't resent—"

"It's understandable," Charlie interrupted, "but you're a grown-ass hockey player, not a child, and you have to know your self-worth. Without the JAR line we wouldn't have made it as far as we did last season, so own that."

"Okay—"

"Also, your personal life, this wedding, your family heritage, your queer representation, the fact you're hockey freaking royalty, you need to stow all of that with your suit in your locker. Now, do you have a problem with doing that, because I've seen it before, and without sounding harsh, if you're not one hundred percent focused on the game then you're letting yourself down, as well as your team."

"I want to—"

"So in conclusion, my door is always open, the team counselor is two doors down if you think that will help."

I think my jaw dropped and I stared at Charlie for the longest time. In the space of five minutes I'd had revelations about Jacob being my best friend, Tate being an issue, and me able to acknowledge my head wasn't in the game. *Damn he's good.*

"Thank you," I said, and slowly backed out of the room in case he had any last minute pearls of wisdom to throw my way. The first thing I did was find an empty office and shut the door, scrambling to yank out my cell phone and dialing the only person I wanted to talk to right now.

Jacob didn't answer, but I knew he was in meetings. "Jacob, you're my best friend, and I love you. That's all I wanted to say. I love you, Jacob, and I can't wait to marry you." Next, I hurried down to the locker room and found Alex, grabbed his arm and ushered him into the weight room. Vlad was in there doing reps, but with one curious glance at me he disappeared.

"What's wrong?" Alex asked, and I winced when I got a good look at his closed expression.

"How is the bruised rib?"

Alex touched over his heart. "Nothing I can't handle."

"Sorry, dude," I offered, and tucked an errant curl behind my ear. "For letting the line down, for messing with the game, for that…" I gestured at his chest, and he shook his head and chuckled.

"You're an idiot." We fist-bumped, then bro-hugged, and after much backslapping I went off to find Tate. He was pacing the video room, never touching the walls or chairs and all the while staring at the screen replaying a shift early on in the Boston game.

"Hey, Tate, whatcha looking for?"

Tate stopped dead and stared at the screen, gesturing me over. "See, look at that line. See how the C is shadowing that move I made? That's insane, but I've been thinking and I know we can get over that in the next game."

"Should have won the last one," I muttered. "Sorry."

Tate didn't appear fazed. "Whatever, we win, we lose, we do all that and we can still lift the cup because we have the rest of the year." Tate glanced at me. "You okay?"

I could have told him a lot of things, how I was feeling, what was in my head, how I'd built everything in my life up until it was a huge ball of pressure burning in my chest. How jealous I was of him and his talent, and how I wanted to be a combination of him and Ten when I grew up. I didn't say any of that.

"Saw Charlie, I'm good."

We fist-bumped, and without any awkwardness we

began dissecting the Boston defense, and for the first time in a few weeks my head felt clearer. I didn't know what I was worried about. I was getting married, I could fix my game, and Jacob's boss was nothing more than that. Just his boss. I had no reason to be jealous, or think I was less attractive to Jacob because Adam was so... Adam.

Jacob loved *me*. I had demands on my time from my crazy career and I had to calm the hell down and appreciate what he was feeling as well, and I couldn't wait to tell him this newest epiphany in my up-and-down life. After the road trip that was, because right now I needed to put hockey first on the east coast. He was heading to New Mexico with work and we wouldn't be in the same place for two weeks.

Everything would be fine.

EVERYTHING WAS *NOT* FINE.

It was day three of the road trip, and even with a win over Brooklyn I was missing Jacob like a limb. Thank god for Apollo who kept sending little updates on the cabin in the desert, and the caterers, and wasn't pushing the boat out into wild waters. His messages gave me an excuse to call Jacob at whatever time of the day I wanted to, and yesterday's late night conversation had led to hot and heavy phone sex, plus I'd even gotten Jacob to step outside of meetings when I was killing time.

I didn't have to like the way my husband appeared in some of Adam's social media posts, like that morning's Insta-post full of techno-speak and a particularly gorgeous photo of Jacob holding a clipboard. I didn't like that one little bit, but that was work. Right? I was all over the freaking media, so who was I to judge?

Yes, Jacob mentioned his work in our calls, and yes, I talked about what some of the guys were up to, but we stayed away from the A-word. In fact, whenever he mentioned this or that project, he never used the words "Adam asked me" or "Adam said" together, not once. I was so freaking stupid, and because he was accepting how stupid I was, it made me love him even harder.

I called him immediately with the current epiphany circulating in my hard head, and he answered on the first ring.

"Hey, babe," he said, in that distracted I'm-working kind of way.

"Love you," I blurted.

He chuckled. "I love you too. Did you call just to tell me that?"

"That and you work too hard." And there it was, the *Adam* thing rearing its ugly head. "That company works you too hard, asks too much of you."

I heard the sigh, because we'd had this conversation before.

"You mean Adam does? Look, Ry, he's a brilliant man, driven, and he expects his team to be just as driven."

Now that Adam had been brought into the conversation I felt as though I could mention the one thing that I'd never said before.

"I saw your photo on his 'gram," I was cautious in the way I approached this, but what I really wanted to know was if Jacob was okay with what was happening. There was something in the way Adam looked at Jacob, even when I was in the room, that gave me a bad feeling, which in turn fed into my stupid jealousy.

"The one with the clipboard? Yeah, I saw that, don't like it, but social media is part of the job."

"You on *his* social media? Looking all hot and sexy, like he got you to pose for him."

Another sigh. "Jeez, Ry, I promise you have nothing to worry about. It's all legit, and I love my work. He's never once acted inappropriately, and he respects me. Anyway, I'm with you, and I love you, and hey, we're getting married soon. So, how did Apollo get on with the ten thousand fairy lights?"

Just like that we were back on our wedding, and Jacob sounded so relaxed and happy that I forgot about Adam and his posting of the sexy photo. It was probably just me who found the photo sexy—because I found everything about Jacob sexy.

Everything was back on an even keel with Jacob, and hockey was good. We beat Boston and, even though it was a hard-fought game, the JAR line worked in perfect sync. We took that same energy to Philly and got our third win in a row, and with those under our belt we were safely in the middle of the table. The only elephant in the room was the honeymoon, and the timing of everything. We were getting married on Valentine's Day, which was also the first day of bye week, straight after the All-star game. Tate was a shoo-in for repping our team, and I was relieved it wouldn't be me and I could concentrate on the wedding. Every team had a week off at some point in February, and we'd planned it perfectly so we'd get at least a few nights on our own in the cabin.

We hadn't organized a honeymoon, given we were getting married on Valentine's Day and I was back to work a few days after, but in the summer we were going to make up for lost time. I'd take him somewhere like France, with a farm, and a jacuzzi, and we'd make love every day and reaffirm how much we meant to each other.

"Earth to Ryker?" Alex snapped his fingers in front of my face and I reeled back, almost falling into the groin of Coach Carmichael who was standing directly behind me. Had the television time-out ended without me realizing? Nope, we were still waiting, but it seemed Alex wanted to talk. "You thinking about the wedding again?"

"No way, I'm totally about the hockey," I lied, then glanced up at the clock, thirty seconds left and we were only one goal ahead of a feisty New York team. All we needed to do was keep hold of the game and block them getting past Colorado. The time out counted down and Coach tapped my line out first, and we headed into the last few moments of hockey with one thing in mind—stop the red, white, and blue from getting past us.

So it was crap when their star forward circled Vlad in a highlight reel move, set loose a goal that dribbled past Colorado's glove, and suddenly we were facing three goals each and heading into overtime.

Well, shit.

JACOB

LYING ON THE SOFA, LAPTOP OPEN BUT UNHEEDED ON MY thighs, I watched, riveted, as the Raptors squared off against New York. Both teams were challengers this year, working through rebuilds that had whittled down older players to make way for youth. New York had lost a long-time beloved goalie, which was always tough for the fans and players alike. But now they had this manic Russian tender, just twenty-two, who was making all the bookies in Vegas rethink their earlier predictions about who would be in the Cup finals come May. The game was tight, three goals each side, and both nets held determined goalies.

"... showdown of the Goalies, Walt! Colorado, the elder goalie versus Ivan Yahantov, the brash young stallion, has been exactly the kind of game we'd predicted in our pregame show."

"It sure has been, Kenny! Both goalies have been tight in net despite what the scoreboard says. With every point crucial now for both teams, this is going to be one heck of a final three. And

not to be forgotten, tonight's final three is sponsored by our friends at the Tuscan Bottled Water Company. Looks like the Raptors are going to send out the JAR line for this faceoff. Not what I'd expected at all!"

"Not me either, Walt. I would have bet on Collins taking the faceoff but it looks like that will fall on Madsen."

"Quite a risk given how shaky Madsen has been of late."

"Fuck you, Kenny. Ryker is anything but shaky!" I barked as I blindly reached for my can of soda on the side table. My phone buzzed with an incoming text. I fished for the cell between the cushions, expecting a call from my mother to quadruple-check their flights. Yes, the wedding was still four weeks away. Yes, she had called to verify airlines and hotels a dozen times. Yes, she was already thinking about what to pack. She might have been more nervous than Ryker and I were, but it was just how Mom ran.

I was in the same place two nights later, sitting on my sofa when the Raptors went up against the Railers in the last of their east coast road trip games. Of course, since they'd lost to New York no one held out hope of them winning against the Railers, and boy did the pundits like that. Particularly any time that Ryker and Ten were on the ice together for any reason. Still, it was a good game and went to a tie, and into overtime.

My cell vibrated across the coffee table, and seeing Adam's name and number flash up, I groaned. Could I just ignore it? I *really* wanted to watch the game. It was an important one for the Raptors, and for Ryker. Eying the text, I blew out a breath that billowed my cheeks.

The text was simple and to the point. Late numbers were in on the final moisture analysis for Bygenta BG Triple Grow. That was good news, but what wasn't so good was the extra part of the message which insisted we needed to collate the data and ended with the question as to when I could get to him. Actually, it sounded less like a question and more of an order. Then another text came in. This one left no room for misunderstanding. *Come to my place, now.*

"God damn it," I huffed, glancing at the TV in time to see that Ryker had already taken the faceoff and was locked in a corner with that dark-haired winger that all the NY fans were crazy about. I slapped my laptop shut and hit Adam back. I sent him an answer to say I'd be there in twenty, but his reply came back so fast I imagined he'd had it ready to send.

Save the gas. I've ordered a car for you and I'm stirring up a pitcher of Sea Breezes to celebrate. ~ A

Seriously. We're drinking during a business meeting? And he already sent a car? What if I said no. Not that I would say no.

Shut up, hick boy. People drink during business meetings all the time. I began to type my concerns, then realized I was probably being an idiot, and deleted it, before sending the lamest answer ever.

Sounds good.

That was a lie. It didn't sound good. A night off to watch hockey and fiddle around with the seating arrangements for the reception sounded good. Apollo had been hounding me for two days for the seating plans. Did it matter where people sat? Seemed it did to Apollo, and since he was doing this all for free, I didn't complain too much. The ceremony was going to be incredible, smaller than Ryker had wanted but larger than I had. Compromise. It worked wonders. We'd have two days in the desert alone which was short, sure, but come summer we had big travel plans that included a trip to the UK to chill with Seb and Alex then France and Germany. As I'd never been outside the States other than a few tourneys in Canada, I was stoked to see Europe over the summer if Ryker was up for it. We had time to plan it all out. But that honeymoon would never happen if I didn't get the seating plans to Apollo. Henry's boyfriend would flay me alive and no one wanted that, least of all me.

I took a few minutes to watch the game go into overtime then snapped the set off. Sighing, I jogged out to the parking lot to meet Adam's driver. The Raptors radio announcers would be hashing it up over the flubs from the team and how we couldn't afford to keep dropping games. It was an everlasting loop. The guys were aware, as were the fans. The car reached the gates, and we cruised into to the mansion, a yellow half-moon high in the dark desert sky.

Adam was right there to greet me, this time in swim trunks, sandals, and a flowy sort of robe that looked like it'd come out of Colorado's closet. The car pulled away. Adam gave me a hug, tugging me into his bare chest, his hands tight to my back. It made me uneasy, his front smashed into mine, but I smiled and gave him a hug in return. Touchy-feely sorts made me wince. My family wasn't into hugs and kisses, not really. Dad rarely displayed emotions, as was the norm in rural farming communities. Men just didn't hug each other. Mom, on the other hand, was more expressive but that was accepted. I wiggled free then felt stupid for doing so. I needed to get over my corn-fed ways.

"You're so cute when you blush," Adam said then patted my cheek. "Tell me you brought trunks." I shrugged and shook my head as my face grew warmer. "Ah well, no problem. I stocked the cabanas with several varieties that should fit." He pulled back, gave me a long up and down, and then draped an arm around my neck. "I like how easily flustered you get. It's an innocent vibe that isn't seen much anymore. Vastly appealing."

He talked as we cut through the dimly lit mansion around to the pool area. There sat the table we'd brunched at a few weeks ago, with a pitcher of cocktails, several fluttering candles, and a platter of what looked to be oysters.

"Marta ran these over a few minutes ago," he said with a wave of his hand. The gold ring on his right index finger glittered under the soft lights surrounding the pool. "She's a lifesaver. Why don't you go change into some trunks? Then we'll swim, sup, and sip!"

"But we're supposed to be collating—"

"We will, relax. Life isn't all work and no play, Jacob." He nudged me toward a blue and white tent, a cabana he'd called it. "Go, get changed! It'll be fine."

It didn't feel fine. It felt off, like *way* off. But then again I was just some farm hick who was far too uptight. Adam, and several others, had mentioned how stiff I was at times. So, shaking off the weirdness, I slipped into the cabana. It had been placed over a solar light so that the interior was illuminated. There on a bench were four different kinds of trunks, all in different colors. I skipped over the Speedo. Yeah, that was a big no. The other three had more material. I went with a blue pair. After tugging off the tag I stripped and hurriedly yanked the trunks over my bare ass. They fit. I folded my clothes and placed them on the bench then slid out of the tent.

"Wow," Adam called as I padded closer. "You're a big brute of a man."

I chuckled self-consciously. "Years of chucking square bales pays off."

"Yes, yes it does. Want a drink?"

"Please."

I sat at the table; shoulders rounded against the slight chill of the night. Adam sat beside me, again, and handed me a tall glass filled to the rim with cranberry juice, grapefruit juice, lime, and vodka. It was much stronger than the last ones I'd had here. I coughed as vodka warmed my belly.

"So, uhm, should we be looking at those numbers?" I asked between nervous gulps.

Adam smiled at me then sat forward, his knee brushing mine. "We have all night. Remember what I told you about relaxing a bit. You're always so tight. Would you like me to rub your shoulders?"

"No!" His eyes flared. "I mean, no, thanks. I'm good."

"So, tell me, have you given my offer any further thought?" He asked as if the answer didn't matter, his gaze flickering down to my chest then tracking to my mouth. I tossed back half my drink while wishing I hadn't left my shirt back in the cabana.

"The one about vacationing in Switzerland?" I asked, eying the pool. Maybe we should swim. That way he couldn't see naked me. The whole vibe here tonight was creeping me out.

"That's the one." He placed his hand on my bare thigh. I stared at it as if it were a scorpion resting on my leg and he moved it away. "But also there's more. You'd love it in Switzerland, you know. And once you were in the program your career would know no bounds. If I can lure you there we can introduce you to the heads of research. Smart man like you shouldn't be slaving away in some university lab. You should be in Europe. That's where the big money research is taking place. With a little help from a friend, we could probably get Bygenta to pick up the tab for your classes, as long as you signed on with Basel Bygenta after you graduated. There's an incredible campus in town with a top notch agriculture department. You could get your master's in sustainable agriculture with an eye on rangeland and animal production then be pipelined right into Bygenta at a much higher wage level."

I sat dumbfounded, staring at him over my Sea Breeze. "I don't know..."

"I know, it's a lot to take in. Hey, maybe you'd rather specialize? Something in crops or mammalian toxicology?" My eyes widened. Adam grinned, his hand coming to rest on my thigh again. "Sue me, I might have stolen a look at your academic files. You aced that measly little toxicology class you had at Owatonna. Imagine what you could do with Bygenta Agrochemicals behind you?

You could push forward the study of toxins in farming and how they affect livestock. I'd be happy to let you live with me at the chalet while you studied. Handsome, intelligent young man like you could probably graduate early. Say three years and then be immediately taken into the Bygenta family."

He squeezed my thigh.

"That's all... wow," I stammered.

Adam leaned closer, his blue gaze dipping to my mouth then coming back up. "'Wow' is right. What do you think, Jacob? A brighter future is just a yes away."

"I'm going to have to think on it and talk it over with Ryker." Adam rolled his eyes then nudged my drink closer. "It's too big of a decision to make without time to consider," I explained as he nodded in disinterest, his gaze still on my mouth.

I downed my cocktail, suddenly parched beyond reason. Adam refilled it as I stammered on about couples.

"Right yes, I recall being part of a couple. But in all honesty, if Ryker loved you as he claims he wouldn't hold you back from such an amazing opportunity, now would he?"

His fingers tightened on my thigh. "It's not that..." I replied, my head starting to feel a little gummy. Shit. How did one damned Sea Breeze fuck me up so fast? Not that I was a party animal but I liked beer. And I sure as hell could hold my booze better than... "What proof is this?"

Adam chuckled, his hand creeping higher. "It's top shelf. You look a little pale."

"Stop touching me," I snapped, slapping at his hand as I went to stand. My knees buckled and the backyard swam.

I stumbled to the left, grabbing at the edge of the table. It flipped with all my weight on it, the pitcher of cocktails flying to the cement with a crash.

"Whoa, big man. You look like you need a bed," he said, his voice wavering and foggy to my ears. He wrapped an arm around me. I leaned into him, unable to focus on anything but the odd sensation of feeling leaving my body. We made it inside, to a long chaise in a dimly lit office before my knees went out. Adam managed to get me into the chaise with a grunt. He sat beside me, stroking my hair and whispering things that I couldn't comprehend before I passed out.

I came to later, much later, and Adam was there, looming over me. My thoughts were cloudy and I tried to sit up but my body hadn't gotten the message from my sloppy brain.

"Easy now, here, have a drink." He held another drink out to me. I lashed out, knocking the glass from his hand. He glowered at me. "I'm getting tired of cleaning up your messes. Now just lay back and let me take care of you."

He grabbed at my crotch.

"What the fuck are you doing!"

He started to reply, but I'd gotten to my feet. The room spun. He stepped closer, touched my face, and I drew back and punched him as hard as a man with rubber arms could punch. He crashed to his ass, blood spewing out of his nose.

"I quit, you sick bastard!"

"Fuck you, you're fired, you ungrateful bastard!" He sat on the floor, holding his face in his hands. "You'll never work on another research project again!"

I tripped over my feet to the back door, found my phone and clothes in the cabana, and somehow managed to dress before I bumbled my way to the front gate and out onto the winding desert road. Fingers still numb from whatever he'd slipped into my drink, I dialed Ryker, praying that he was home now and would save me. Someone had to...

6

RYKER

Seeing Ten opposite Tate on this final faceoff was surreal. There was only a minute left of OT in this game and so far it had been the Railers who'd had the upper hand, until it seemed, Tate turned up the speed and took advantage of a gassed Ten.

We had a chance, the puck heading toward a very determined Stan, and when the puck dribbled free of a mess of men hassling for it in the corner, I caught it on my stick, shuttled it back to Alex, and took up position near the net, ready for a tip-in, if Alex managed to pass it to Tate through a tight Railers' defense. I didn't remember much past Tate collecting the disc of rubber on his stick then flexing back for what was going to be one of his famed slap shots. It felt as if the entire Railers' arena was frozen in time and the expectation was real.

Tate let the puck fly just as a D-man got pushed into my space and made me stumble out of position.

The puck slammed into my mask at one hundred

miles an hour, which even with the padding I wore, freaking hurt. At the last moment I'd been shoved into the wrong place at the wrong time by an overenthusiastic Adler Lockhart, and the fact that the missile came off a fast-as-fuck slapshot from Tate Collins just added insult to injury. I went down onto the ice like a felled tree, my skates going from under me, my entire body sliding onwards into the boards, thankfully side-first.

My first thought, after the initial pain and stars, was that Jacob and my mom were watching this live on television, not to mention Dad at the Railers' bench. Even as my team and the medic crowded around me, I waved a hand to let people know I was okay. They'd have seen me go down and it would be an awful reminder of what had happened to Ten.

"I'm okay," I said to the nearest person I could find, but I must have been speaking in tongues, because it was Tate crouching right there and he was frowning. "I'm okay," I repeated. Ten was there as well, I saw his worried expression and gave him a weak smile.

We need to get him off the ice, can he move?

Do we need to get a stretcher?

No fucking way was I being dragged off this ice lying on my damn back. I rolled onto my side, my brain shaken, eyes hurting, and felt as though I was going to vomit. I didn't know where the puck had hit me, but I could taste the iron saltiness of blood, and I pulled up a fist to cover my mouth, my tongue worrying at a loose tooth.

Oh well, I guess if I had to lose a tooth it had to be at the hands of the league player with the second fastest slapshot on record. People moved to help me stand, Tate on one side, repeating the word *shit* over and over, and Alex on the other. Between them holding me, and my own stubborn Madsen determination, I made it to the exit past the bench and even acknowledged the stick taps against the boards from both teams. I glanced a look at Dad who seemed way too pale, his lips thin and his brow creased in worry. I gave him a brief nod, as the crowd clapped and hollered their respect. It was bloodthirsty, but fans loved the drama of a good puck to the mouth, and respected a player for taking the beating and blood loss. Go figure.

I made it all the way into the tunnel, far from prying eyes, where Alex and Tate had handed me off to Raptors medical staff, plus the on-site Railers' medics.

"Talk to me," Eddie demanded as I shook off my gloves and pretended everything was okay. Eddie was our traveling medic, the one who spoke directly to management and coaches and the same one who could can a guy for losing blood. Not that I wanted to lose blood.

"I need to call Jacob," I said although the words were garbled, and the pain was kicking into overdrive.

My tongue slipped over the loose tooth and it wobbled free, and I held my hand under my chin as it fell out, along with way too much blood. This was my first tooth lost to hockey, and I guess it had a story to go with it. I could tell my grandkids how the famous Tate Collins had used me for target practice, and they'd be all goggle-eyed as Jacob ruffled my now gray curls and told them not to listen to Grandpa Ryker's war stories.

Okay, I'm losing my shit here.

They took me through concussion protocol, gave me four stitches for the split lip, and packed my tooth in a baggie and put it into my locker. I didn't know what they wanted me to do with it, maybe immortalize it as the-tooth-that-Tate-knocked-out or something equally stupid.

Is it just me or is it hot in here?

"I want to go back out," I slurred, whatever pain meds they gave me were twisting their way around my words, and I felt tired.

"You're done, Ryker," Eddie said, not unkindly.

"Did the game finish?" We were in overtime, right?

Eddie sighed. "The puck hit you and then hit the pipes. When they restarted, the Railers had momentum. They scored."

"That's shit." I placed a hand to my cheek—I'd taken a puck to the mouth for no reason. I'd have to make an appointment with the team surgeon, get some X-rays on my jaw, but first I needed to make sure my mom knew in case she was still worried. The entire Raptors team trooped in, on a low from losing, and I slipped into the corridor before they could talk to me, still sweaty and in uniform, my skates the only thing I'd taken off, apart from my gloves.

As I expected there was a text from my mom asking for details, which I replied to straight away, reassuring her I'd lost a tooth but it was okay. She sent back a thumbs-up but she was a hockey daughter, a former hockey wife, and mom to me, so she knew the score. Teeth never lasted long in hockey, but thankfully this was one at the back and my sometimes-vain self could handle that.

I didn't see a message from Jacob to say that he'd seen the incident and was worried, so I sent him a text, and messages in the other apps we had going on, but there was no sign he was online. Maybe he'd turned off after I got knocked down and… and what? He said he was going to be watching, but I guess he'd fallen asleep over work again. At least he'd see the messages in the morning so I wasn't too worried.

"Hey," Dad said from the corridor behind me, poking his head outside the Railers locker room door.

"Hey," I forced a ton of enthusiasm into that single word.

"How many?" he asked.

"Just the one," I gave weak jazz hands.

"N'awww," came Ten's voice, and he poked his head around the corner by Dad. "My baby lost his first tooth."

"Fuck off, asshole," I said with a smile, and then gave Ten the finger.

Ten fake-clutched his pearls. "Kids these days," he said in a falsetto and batted his lashes.

Dad shoved him back into the room and followed him with a wave. At least they had a win to discuss. I went back into the locker room, expecting it to be into the middle of a tirade from Coach Carmichael, but it was calm in there and I took my spot.

Coach had left the speech for me to arrive and we all looked at him expectantly.

"Now what you played there," he indicated toward the

door that led to the tunnel. "That was the best hockey I've seen from you this season. Keep it up."

He walked out of the room and Colorado shook his head. "Seems to me, Ryker, you need to lose a tooth every game just so we play right." Everyone stared at him, then at me, and then the laughing started and we didn't stop for a long time.

By the time the plane landed back in Tucson I was done. My jaw wasn't fractured, but I had a doozy of a black eye, and a throbbing pain I had to live with if I didn't want to give into the temptation of the stronger drugs. I'd seen enough of my dad's generation hooked on painkillers to know what effect that had, and had talked at length with Dieter whenever he was at one of Dad's Summer barbecues. He'd struggled with an addiction to pain pills, and I knew how easy it was to get sucked into the cycle of pain relief.

Still, I was grumpy and tired, but I wasn't driving home, depending on a lift from Alex, who dropped me at my place and then drove off with a smile and a wave. Jacob still hadn't returned my texts, but it was three in the morning now, and I'd bet he was still asleep on the sofa. The thought of snuggling next to him and having him kiss my booboo better gave me a spring in my step, and I jogged to the elevators mashing the button to our floor and darting out sideways as soon as the doors opened. I didn't find Jacob asleep on the sofa though. In fact, he wasn't anywhere. His laptop was missing, his phone, his favorite Raptors' jacket with my number on the arm, but nowhere could I find a note in explanation as to where he'd gone.

Without thinking I called his phone, but it went to voicemail and I left a message that was ten percent pissed and ninety worried. I'd bet he was working; he knew I was coming home tonight, and that it would be super late, but he always waited up. Or at least he'd be on the sofa asleep, where he'd been waiting and had given into his exhaustion. He worked too hard, and I had this horrible premonition that he was up at three a.m. in the office working on some seed stat with *Adam*.

Okay, stow the jealousy, get some Tylenol, and think.

Sometime around four, just as I thought I should call the hospitals, and after I'd talked to Adam who reassured me he hadn't seen Jacob, I began pacing the apartment, had 911 on my phone, ready to call in any and all favors to find out where Jacob was, but my phone began ringing obnoxiously loud, and Jacob's name flashed on the screen.

"Where the hell are you?" I blurted out rather than say hello, or how are you, or I love you.

"Ry," he sounded weird, as if he'd been shouting and his voice was hoarse. He didn't sound like *my* Jacob.

"What's wrong? Where are you?" I asked again, this time more controlled, and with a hell of a lot more worry.

"I need you to come get me, Ry. From the gate outside Adam's place."

I glanced at his truck parked where it belonged.

"Where are you? Are you okay?"

"Just come get me."

"I'm on my way, stay on the phone." I couldn't bear the pain in Jacob's voice—I thought my big strong man was going to cry, and it'd been a long time since he'd cried. I took the stairs down to the parking lot and climbed into my car. Within minutes I was out on the road in the dark, the clock showing four forty-two a.m., my head pounding, and the pain in my jaw making me wince. "Are you still there?" I asked, begged, pleaded, and I heard him say yes. But it sounded wrong.

Everything was wrong.

I floored the car as soon as I was able, wondering what I would say if a cop pulled me over and not giving any actual shits if they did. I made it to Adam's in record time, saw Jacob standing on the side of the road. I screeched to a halt and clambered out of the car.

"What happened?" I checked him over as I ran to him, and held him, and then he guided me back to the car.

"Fuck," he yelled as soon as the door was shut. "Fuck, fuck, fuck!"

He was nursing his fist, and before the interior light switched off, I could see his knuckles were bruised. Oh shit, had he gotten into a fight with Adam? Killed him? My head spun as I calculated how long it would take to get to the border, and then get over without ID, and how much money I could get my hands on, and I'd done all that before Jacob turned to me and shook his head.

"I didn't kill him. But I hit him. Hard. And I quit." I reached out and closed my hand around his bruised fist. "Shit, Ryker, I quit."

"What happened?"

"I don't have a fucking clue." Jacob coughed.

"Jacob?"

"I don't know," he shouted, then scrubbed at his eyes. "I think he roofied me, but I put him straight about the job, that's all that matters."

Roofied? What the fuck? I opened the car door and started to climb out. "I'm going to kill him."

Jacob yanked me back. "Leave it, Ry. Take me home." I hesitated, because there was too much anger in me to leave it there. "Please. Just take me home," he added quietly.

So with reluctance, but with love and fear for Jacob, I did what he asked.

7

JACOB

BY THE TIME I WAS BACK HOME, I FELT LIKE A GOLEM.

No, that wasn't right. Golems have no feelings, and I was having lots of those. Maybe I wished I were made of clay so the swirling, horrible emotions that were about to overtake me wouldn't be crushing my chest. I'd just be cold. Like clay. Right now, being a clay man would have been good. Ryker touched me, just lightly on the arm, and I lifted my head to look at him. He had a split lip with stitches, a black eye, and I imagined it must've been so painful, but he acted as if it didn't matter. That was all it took. I fell into him, desperate for a loving touch, terrified over the time gap in my head, and sickened at the thought that Adam had not only played me like a fiddle but could've touched me in ways that…

"I feel sick," I groaned as I clung to Ryker. He felt so good, so right…

"Okay, babe, okay, let me grab you a bucket."

"No, don't leave just… hold me," I whimpered. And so

he did. He held me up until his smaller frame couldn't support me anymore.

"Let's sit, just sit, I'll go make coffee. Call the cops."

"No, fuck no, don't call the cops!" I tumbled to the sofa, my head bumping the back, my gut roiling, my world upside down.

"Jacob, that motherfucker drugged you!" Ryker snarled as I waved a hand around in weak circles.

"No cops… just, babe, coffee please."

He worried at his stitches but did as asked. In the time it took to brew a cup of coffee, I'd laid down and drawn my knees into my stomach. I still felt queasy, and my brain was scrambling to delve into the void of last night.

"Here, sip," Ryker whispered, kneeling beside me as he held a straw to my lips. I sucked slowly, the hot liquid coating my throat, then my belly. "Let me get your shoes off."

I said nothing. Once my sneakers hit the floor, Ryker sat beside me. Maybe an hour or two passed with us that way, me on my side with silent tears leaking onto the couch cushion, Ryker entreating me to drink some coffee and eat crackers which was all I could keep down. He didn't push me to talk about it, he was simply there when I needed him the most, and I willed myself to pick up my head so he could sit on the couch. Once my cheek rested on his thigh, he began carding his fingers through my hair. Each time he did it I picked up the smell of chlorine. Had I been swimming? What the fuck had happened?! Why would Adam do such a thing? I'd trusted him, even looked up to him. And he'd been a fucking predator, a wolf, circling whom he had obviously known was a dull-witted deer.

"You were right," I coughed out sometime around eight at night after spending all day on the couch. Ryker hushed me. I shuddered and sniffled, as guilt and shame took up residence in my breast. "You were right to distrust him."

"Don't make this about being right or wrong, babe. He's a creep and the cops will agree."

I ignored the cops comment—the thought of telling other people what had happened wasn't worth facing right now. "He knew I was stupid, gullible…"

"Hey no, you are *not* gullible, not at all!" Ryker's fingers continued their gentle stroking of my hair and temple. "You're a warm, trusting man. This is not your fault, Jacob. It's his, and he will pay for doing this!"

His anger flowed out of him. I squeezed my eyes shut. "I hit him. He'll ruin me, Ry. I won't be able to get another job in ag research ever again." My gut cramped. Ryker leaned over to press his lips to my brow. "I should have listened to you. I'm such a damned fool."

"No you're not. You're a loving soul with an open heart. That asshole saw that and took advantage of it. This all rests on him." A moment passed. "Why don't you start at the beginning and tell me what you do remember?"

I told him, all of it, or all of which I could dredge up. The table flipping… the pitcher smashing on the concrete and then… nothing. Nothing until I came to and Adam was hovering over me, touching my arm as if he had a right to. I had to fight back the urge to gag.

Eventually, I quieted and somehow I fell into a fitful

sleep. When I woke from a strange, empty sort of dream, I sat up and was happy to see that the room stayed in place. The sun was high in the sky, noonish or so I guessed, and Ryker was out on the balcony talking to someone on his cell in just a pair of cutoff denim shorts. The door was cracked, so I could hear his side of the conversation as I massaged my temples. I had a headache tiptoeing around the inside of my skull. Stress, for sure, and perhaps a remnant of the drug Adam had dosed me with.

"… yeah, no, I can get him there. Yeah, thanks so much. I owe you big time, Sharpy."

I stood, easing to my feet, and padded slowly to the door. Ryker glanced at me with such compassion in his hazel eyes I nearly lost my control. Instead, I swallowed down the ball of feels and stepped outside.

"Hey," he said, slipping his phone into his back pocket. "How do you feel?"

"Mm, weird. Like… like I'd traveled through time but jumped some hours. Or flown through a few dozen timelines. Who were you talking to?" I asked, looking out over Tucson. The sun on my face felt good. My insides were still cold and clammy.

"I was thinking we should get some tests—"

"I don't want to go to a hospital—"

"I spoke to Sharpy, the trainer for the Raptors, he said he'd help."

"The fuck? You told some random guy—"

"No, he's *Sharpy*, we can trust him."

"I don't like it."

Ryker stood next to me. I glanced his way. The wind plucked at some curls. He had dark bags under his eyes.

Had he slept at all? "Babe, you should get some testing done and get checked out." I shivered. Ryker slipped closer, his arm coming around my back. I closed my eyes and let my head fall to rest on his. "You need to know things."

Things. Like if I'd been given an STD of some kind. Fuck. I wanted to hide in a closet at the same time I wanted to go find Adam and beat him into a coma.

"I don't think he did… *that* to me," I whispered into the soft desert wind. "I don't feel…"

Ryker hugged me tight. "It's okay, you don't have to talk about it now, but you do need to be tested and have a doctor check you out. Sharpy, Kevin Sharp, you remember him. Big guy, red hair, a wicked sense of humor. He's willing to do the testing. He runs them on us players all the time. We can go to the barn whenever you're ready. I'll be with you the whole time he does the tests."

How the hell had this become my life? Why had I been so fucking trusting? God, I was a moron.

"Okay yeah, I just… want to shower first."

"Maybe you shouldn't."

"Fuck, Ry."

He hugged me hard and held me up, held my hand, held my heart and soul as we snuck into the arena like thieves. There was no official practice today but there would be players in the building as it wasn't unknown for Coach to call in players for one-on-one chats. Ryker had pre-empted that, but he'd exaggerated and said he had a stomach bug, and would let Coach know if the doc said he was going to be at practice the next day. I knew what he was doing—giving himself the option of staying with me, and that was another shit thing to happen in a list of shit things.

A silent but sorrowful Sharpy drew the blood. He never once asked why I hadn't gone to the hospital or the cops, he just carefully tended to me. Then there were swabs placed in places where no swab should ever go. Followed by an exam that left me wanting to bury my head in the sand and never extract it. I hated it and I hated myself for being such a sheep. I'd owned cattle with more common sense than I had displayed. I should have never gone to his place alone. I should have picked up on the same things Ryker had picked upon.

"Hey, don't go there, okay?" Ryker said. I nodded but my brain kept trucking along those same rutted roads of regret. "We'll have your results in a few hours. Sharpy already said that there were no signs of assault and…"

He drifted off.

"Yeah, thank God."

After thanking the Raptors' trainer we slipped out through the back exit, nodding at the security guard who was stationed there. Luckily, we ran into no one. Ry insisted on stopping at a local chicken shack for takeout. I rode along, uncaring about the smell of herbs and spices even though my stomach was gurgling with hunger. Once we were home, I showered, scrubbing myself clean with such vigor my skin ached when I ran a towel over it.

"Come sit and eat," Ryker said the moment I stepped into the kitchen in a T-shirt and worn fleece shorts.

He piled a plate full of chicken breasts, mashed potatoes, and coleslaw. He was wolfing down tenders and fries, his worried gaze on me as I forked up some spuds. The gravy wasn't as good as Mom's and the slaw was a little old-tasting, but I dove into the food ravenously. Each time I would glance up, Ryker smiled at me and passed along another buttermilk biscuit. Halfway through our meal I took a small milk break. Ry wiped his fingers on some paper towels.

"What?" I asked when he stared at me.

He blinked. "I just… I want you to know that I love you."

"I love you, too."

"I've been thinking, and if you want to postpone the wedding I would totally get it."

"Is that what you want?" Would he ever want me that way again? Was Ryker having second thoughts? Was this going to destroy everything?

"Fuck no, I'm thinking of you," Ryker said with passion.

"No. No way in hell does Adam get to ruin our day. The fucker already tanked my career, he is *not* getting the pleasure of fucking up our wedding!"

Ryker reached out to take my hand. My fingers curled around his. "I'm glad to hear that fight in your voice. When I found you… and then when we came home… I was scared for you."

"It was bad." I had to admit. My phone buzzed. Checking it I saw it was the lab calling back with my results. I threw Ryker a worried look. "Test results."

"We got this." He squeezed my fingers.

Unable to draw a deep breath, I took the call and listened as the tech read off each negative result. She did mention that there were still some rather large traces of GHB in my blood, and that it indicated a lot had been used. She also mentioned that if the same dosage had been used on a smaller man or a woman it would have put them into a coma. That was some shit. I didn't know how to process that other than feeding the anger that was building inside me. That *asshole*. He had to be stopped before he killed someone.

"All negative, okay, thank you so much," I told the technician. She said it was her pleasure. I thanked her a few more times, hung up, and cried one more time right into my slaw. Ryker left his seat to gather me close. He was emotional too as I passed along the GHB info. We were both half-mad with relief.

"We're going to run out of paper towels," he teased after we gathered ourselves a bit. It took some cold water to the face combined with lots of nose blowing but we returned to our meals, and some cursing when Ryker caught his lip as he wiped himself. "So what the hell did he do when you were out if he didn't... you know?"

I shrugged, my head so full of outlandish ideas and emotions, I couldn't concentrate on anything sensible.

"I don't know. Maybe he just..." I made the hand motion for jerking off. Ryker's face blanched but he said nothing, just shoved a tender into his mouth as his eyes glittered with fury. "I'm going to call human resources at the college. They have to be made aware of what kind of monster they have roaming around campus."

"As soon as you've finished eating, and you feel... right."

"I'm not sure I ever will."

"You will, Jacob, and I'll be right here with you."

"I was so stupid. I can't believe you'd want anything to do with me—"

Ryker spoke right over me. "You said he fired you. That's just from the Bygenta project, right? I mean, he's not in charge of any of the other things that go on there. When you talk to HR or the dean or whoever, surely they have to see that you're the victim in all of this."

"Yeah, well, I hope so."

"Well fuck them if they don't! If they don't back you up we'll buy some land off Colorado and build a farm on it! Then you can have cows and grow corn."

His exuberance and defense of me made my heart swell. "Not sure how well corn grows in sand, but I love that idea. A house, some cows, a dog, a kid or two, and maybe a couple of horses."

"Oh totes on the horses! We could call one No Name and ride him through the desert." That made me snort. He grinned across our greasy meal at me. "I'm serious, babe. Whatever happens I am all about you being happy. We'll make our dreams come true. No creeper is going to stall our future, Jacob."

And in that moment, I had to trust that Ryker had this all figured out because I sure as hell didn't. I *did t*rust the man I loved, though.

8

RYKER

"Can you tell me why you haven't gone to the authorities Mr. Benson?"

Jacob and I had spent hours talking this over, but I couldnt force him to make this real by getting the cops involved.

That didn't stop the head of the college HR department, Lloyd Johnson, from asking. He was a placid man, even at the end of a college day and with a desk full of paperwork. It had been a few days since the assault and Jacob was stoic but shaky, although I think it might only have been me who saw through to the scared man inside. Lloyd shook our hands, asked us to sit, didn't question when we shut the door. I liked him. We'd met once before at a fundraiser, and he'd had only vague words to say to me about hockey, which he didn't really watch, but he had said that Jacob was a new star in the department. In my books he rocked, and the way he spoke was calm, matter-of-fact, hell, even now he was sitting there listening, his eye twitching.

"At least you were tested. Can I see the results?" Lloyd asked after a short pause when Jacob had stopped explaining. Jacob had stuck to the simple facts in that he'd gone to Adam's house for work, drunk something, lost some hours, and had woken to find Adam leering over him and stating all kinds of heinous things. How I kept my cool I didn't know, but it wouldn't last long if Adam were to walk in right now because I might just have shoved him into the wall.

Through the wall.

Jacob passed his phone over, and Lloyd scrolled through the information.

"Do you want me to email this on to you?" Jacob asked when Lloyd jotted down some points on a pad and then passed it back.

"Please. If you could do that I would be grateful." He wrote a few more things and Jacob and I exchanged glances as he cleared his throat and then scribbled something else.

"What next?" I asked when Jacob sat in silence.

"Well, let me get this right. Adam Isaksson called you to attend his *private* residence to discuss *work-related* matters. Upon arrival he *suggested* you change into trunks, and offered you *alcohol*. You asked about the work and he said that would follow, and then you recall falling over, and then waking up on a sofa in Adam Isaksson's residence, having lost time that you can't account for."

Jacob made a sound I'd never heard before, a mix of exhaustion and distress and embarrassment.

"This is not Jacob's fault," I snapped.

Lloyd glanced up from his notes immediately. "Of

course it's not." He kept his tone even, but with a look he implied I should let him finish, so I subsided into my chair.

What I wanted was the cops, the FBI, and every single NHL enforcer with sticks, hunting down Adam and making him pay for hurting Jacob, but I had to sit on my hands for a moment. I felt sick, and lightheaded, and completely out of control. Jacob and I were walking in a dazed nightmare, where none of this seemed real.

"What do you want me to do?" Jacob asked and reached out to hold my hand.

"You've quit the independently funded Bygenta program."

"Yes."

"And you physically assaulted Adam."

"Yes." Jacob sounded so miserable.

"And the results show that you ingested GHB."

I didn't want this list to sound so freaking ordinary—like a goddamn shopping list. "Enough GHB that anyone smaller than Jacob could have ended up in a coma, or worse, dead."

Lloyd blinked at me, nodded, then added something to his notes.

"You're aware that the Isaksson foundation is a major benefactor of the college?" he asked.

I'd had enough. Burning with rage, I jumped to my feet. If this asshole was going to choose money over Jacob then we were out of here faster than Tate Collins on a breakaway. "We're going straight to the fucking police and—"

"Please sit down, Mr. Madsen," Lloyd said firmly, and

even though the scarlet mist had descended there was something about his tone and the fact that Jacob hadn't moved which cut through the fury.

"It's okay, Ry." Jacob tugged at my hand and pulled me to sit, which I did with great reluctance and a ton of self-righteous indignation along with a healthy dose of fear.

"It's *not* okay," I snapped. Jacob winced, and just seeing that made me subside into silence because I wasn't the victim here, I was the outsider who needed to stay the hell quiet for a while.

"This needs to be done by the book," Lloyd said, and held up his hand to stop me from interrupting. I guess that was in case I had some explosive comment to add fuel to the already burning situation. I cursed him in my thoughts, and gripped Jacob's hand. "We need to make an official report to the police. Can I ask again why you had independent tests and didn't immediately report this to the authorities?"

Jacob deflated, and I'd never seen him look so defeated. "I'm six-five, I weigh two hundred and fifty pounds, I'm a grown man who should've never been in that position, I'm stupid, mortified, and horrified that I let it get to this. Terrified that I was so wrong in trusting him, and ashamed that I didn't listen to Ryker or my gut." Everything spilled out of him so fast, each syllable dripping with self-hatred and regret, and I burned inside as if I had hell in my heart.

"I could tell you that you shouldn't feel shame at what someone has done to you. But as the victim, and as a man, you have a unique mix of qualities that will make it hard for you to reconcile everything. I'm so sorry, Jacob, that we have let you down, and before we call the authorities I want to apologize on behalf of the University of Arizona." He cleared his throat "Please know that we will be following every policy, procedure, and law, and supporting you regardless of who the other party is or what they may have donated to the college. You are an employee, a friend of the faculty, and this will be taken seriously." He picked up the phone but paused. "We need to get the authorities involved." He was asking Jacob a question and at this point it was Jacob's choice as to what happened next. "Do you want me to call them?"

Jacob glanced at me, and I gave him a smile of what I hoped was reassurance, but probably looked like a grimace. He was still staring at me when he nodded.

"Yes."

I don't recall much of the rest of the day, it passed in a blur of interviews, some at the college and the rest in the station. The worst of it was the accusations wrapped up in questions. How could you let it happen? Were there no signs? Were you trying to seek favor with the *very rich man*? I knew everyone was only doing their job, but it wasn't me who called an end to the latest interview full of pointed questions with a demand for a lawyer. As soon as Jacob said that he felt he needed one, I was straight on the phone to Vlad, who didn't judge, or comment, but said he'd deal with it.

I had to call in the team, they needed to know where my head was, so there was that, but also with the might of the management team in my corner, maybe I could be of more use than just holding Jacob's hand. This issue was going to affect the Raptors when it inevitably linked to me and to one of the richest men in Arizona. It would come back on me, because there was no way I was backing down in my support.

When Vlad arrived at the station he had Marc with him, owner and general manager, plus one of the team lawyers and a whole list of demands that they launched into. I'd never been more relieved to see Vlad, who made a comment about my bruised eye, the stitches in my lip, and the tooth I'd lost to break the uneasy silence that had fallen over the room when it was just us in there. The lawyer and Marc had vanished to do whatever they needed to do, and Jacob was quiet.

"You lost a tooth?" Jacob seemed surprised, and I realized we hadn't even talked about it, and he hadn't touched his phone to check out his texts, or emails. I knew he was trying to avoid Adam, so he wouldn't have seen reports of the game. "I thought you just got a high stick or something. I should have asked you what happened." He cradled my face, and I wanted to cry at the pain in his expression.

"It's nothing, just Tate, a puck, and one of his slapshots, then me minus a tooth," I joked.

"Did you get your jaw X-rayed?"

"Yep."

"And you're okay? Can I do anything?" Typical that the big man was trying to look after *me*.

"You mean put my tooth back?" I hooked a finger in my mouth and showed him the space, but it hurt too much and stretched the stitches so I let go.

He leaned over and pressed a butterfly kiss to my nose. "If I could magic the tooth back I would," he said.

"I just hope there are no scars by the time we have our wedding photos." I touched my lip and winced. "Maybe they can just photograph my good side."

Jacob made an mmm sound and subsided into silence.

"Do you even have a good side?" Vlad joked, and I tried to smile, but Jacob had retreated into himself, taking a seat opposite me and closing his eyes. I didn't like the fact we weren't touching and I moved to sit next to him, and I think Vlad picked up on the new tension that had been added to the already fucked-up situation. He made a show of standing and brushing himself down. "I need to call Tate, he's at a signing today."

"I'm sorry if you were supposed to be there with him," Jacob murmured.

"Me? With Tate the all-American hero and everyone fawning over him?" Vlad huffed a laugh. "Do you know how many people I'd have to kill if they touched him?"

He sketched a wave, and finally it was just me and Jacob in the room. I reached for a hand and gripped it. "I love you." I thought that needed saying.

He squeezed my hand. "Maybe you're right, and we should cancel the wedding," he murmured.

"Wait, I never said I wanted to *cancel* our wedding. I said I understood if you wanted to delay—"

"What if we do cancel?" Jacob turned in his seat to face me, and he was so fierce with his expression. "This could get ugly and you'll be caught up in it—"

"I can handle 'ugly.'"

"What if I don't want you to handle ugly? Huh? I could go somewhere, and this could stay private and no one would have to know you were connected to this at all. Think about your career."

"Okay, I'll think," I said, and tapped my chin with finger. "Okay, here's the thing. If you take one step away from me that isn't to meet in front of an officiator at our wedding, then I will stand on a box in the middle of the city and tell everyone who you are to me. Then when everything hits the fan, they'll all know that my *husband* has me in his corner, along with all of the Raptors fans."

"*All* of the Raptors fans?" Jacob deadpanned.

"I know for a fact we have at least a hundred of those now." In fact, we had thousands with the last few games being sell-outs, but I was going for the joking/serious balance the same as he seemed to be.

"And you're going to stand on a box?" Jacob half smiled—trust him to pick up on the one thing I had no thoughts about before it left my mouth.

"A big box. Or, your shoulders. I could sit there and then we'd be as tall as a sequoia and you do that so well."

"Being a tree?"

"Holding me up I mean. That's what you do, Jacob, you hold me up because you're so strong, but you know what? It's my turn now, so you'd better turn up to the cabin in that tux Apollo found you, so we get married."

"What if the cops want me to—?"

"We have four weeks to the wedding. It's a few hours out of a day if we want it to be. Just us, and we don't even have to be at the cabin if we're needed elsewhere, but whatever happens we *will* fight this."

He clutched my hand, and smiled. "Okay then."

With that settled we sat mostly in silence, and it was a

few hours of stale coffee and old cookies before the door opened and the officer who was running this case came in to talk to us. He was followed by the team lawyer, and a serious Mark, and they sat down.

"Adam Isaksson has voluntarily attended his local station, after a search warrant was executed focusing on computers in his possession. At first glance certain images were found at his residence, including evidence of videos. I'm afraid we can't share much about the case at this time."

"Video of me?" Jacob asked quietly.

"We've only just collected what we can, there's a lot more to go through." The officer didn't drop his gaze once, and I felt the tension in Jacob subside.

"I don't want to see any video of me. Ever. Can we go now?"

It looked as if the cop had something to say but Mark and the team lawyer moved between him and us.

"We're leaving, they've had enough. My car is waiting," Mark said. "Let's go." The cop never said a word.

Hand-in-hand, Jacob and I left the station, following Mark and the lawyer, and I don't know what I expected when I stepped outside but it was nothing like I thought it would be. The weather was the same as when we'd arrived, no one we met in the corridors looked at us differently, the outside world hadn't shifted on its axis.

And I still had Jacob. So everything would be okay.

9

JACOB

Two days later, I woke at four a.m. from a terrifying dream where I was in a pit, à la *Silence of the Lambs*, staring at Adam grinning down at me. I came awake with a scream of horror that woke Ryker and probably half our neighbors. Drenched in sweat, shaking, I got out of the sodden sheets and into the bathroom before I threw up. Ryker knelt beside me, his cool hand moving in soothing circles on my wet back.

"Fuck," I huffed, angry as hell at myself for being so weak. I'd been solid as a rock for the past forty-eight hours. Doing what needed to be done. Work, the cops, pressing on with the wedding despite Ryker's long, worried looks.

"You should talk to someone," he whispered as I dry-heaved. "There's no shame in getting help."

"You help me," I grunted then spit into the toilet, my gut bubbling with stress, anxiety, and fear. I hated that the most. The fear. I'd never been scared before, not really, not since I'd hit six-foot and kept going. Now, I was scared. Of some guy I could beat into paste if I wanted to. It made no sense, but there he was, in my dreams, terrifying me. He'd been charged with a whole ream of things, including video that incriminated him, but that included none of me. If there was some then he'd not kept it, or maybe he didn't record the first night or... *shit.* Talking to someone about what'd happened was a horrific thought.

Ryker kissed my shoulder. "I'm not a professional. Please, baby, talk to the team shrink. Or someone from the college. I know you think you have to be Mr. Stoic all the time, but this kind of shit goes deep. Please, for me? Maybe someone connected to the team?"

I glanced at him hunkered down beside me. I never could refuse the man a damned thing.

"Okay yeah, I'll talk to someone, but not that Charlie guy."

"Cool yeah, no, Charlie is awesome but you need a pro. Let me make some calls. You okay? Want to go back to bed and try to get some sleep?"

"Oh hell no."

So we went to the living room, curled up under a throw, and watched some old *MythBusters* reruns until the sun came up. I held Ryker to me, my nose in his curls, and stared unseeing at the explosions taking place on the screen. I couldn't shake that dream. It lingered in the darkest corner of my mind for hours. It was still with me when I walked into the very feng shui office of Lita Morgan, a sexual assault therapist the college had on staff as part of their Title XI Office and Advocacy group.

Dr. Morgan was a petite woman with a soft speaking

voice and incredibly big brown eyes. She had a tight afro, was maybe hobbit height, and thin as a rail. A strong breeze could've carried her off like a dandelion blow. Her office was all blues and tans and yellows, as were the furnishings. She was dressed casually, a billowy caftan in an African print, and Chucks. I tried to stay focused on why I was there, but as soon as we sat down I had to comment.

"Nice Chucks," I noted.

She smiled and crossed her legs, bouncing that sneaker up and down. "I wear them all the time. High heels suck. Do you like sneakers?"

"Yeah." We had a ten-minute discussion about Nikes, which led to Ryker, who loved sneakers and left them lying all over the apartment. Then we chatted about Ry and me, our pasts, the wedding, and what kind of dog I wanted in the future.

"A herding dog, maybe a red heeler," I said, smiling at the memory of the one we'd had when I was a kid. "Rex. I want a red heeler named Rex. And he could ride out with me and Ryker, once Ryker works up the courage to get on a horse, and we could check the cattle on our ranch. We're going to have a ranch someday. And a dog. Rex. Yeah, Rex would love our kids too. Heelers are great dogs. I wish I had one. They're protective too. Rex would have kept Adam at bay and… and…"

The world kind of collapsed on me and I bent over, covered my face, and cried inconsolably for several minutes. Doctor Morgan kept handing me tissues and telling me to let *it* out, but men weren't supposed to sob like soap opera stars. Men sucked it up. Men got on with it. Men didn't let little mealy shitheads assault them.

"That's not at all the case, Jacob. Sexual assaults happen to both men and women."

Damn it, that was not supposed to have been said out loud.

"There was... he didn't... shit." I blew my nose and shot to my feet, the room feeling considerably smaller than it had ten minutes ago. "He didn't do that to me. I'm not sure what he did... there are videos that he made but I can't..." I walked to the window and looked out over the U of A campus. Students milled around on the lawns, enjoying the second week of January in short sleeves. Back home we'd have been asshole deep in snow. "I miss snow."

"Does snow make you feel safe?"

I plucked at the blind that was at half-mast. "It reminds me of home when I was a kid. My mom making breakfast, me and Dad doing the milking, the cold snap of bitter air in your nose and the calls of the cattle. I miss that."

"You had a good childhood by the sounds."

"The best," I sighed. I turned from the quad to stare at my therapist. "I wanted to give that kind of upbringing to my kids. Then I discovered I was gay, and there was that upset, and then I couldn't keep the farm from being sold. I knew it was my responsibility and we lost our home. And now... now there's this mess. I keep letting my parents down."

She reached over to pat the chair across from her. I shook my head. She patted it again. I huffed then returned to my seat.

"Do you like gingersnaps?"

I blinked at her. Cookies? We were talking cookies after I dropped an emotional nuke not five seconds ago?

"Uhm, sure yeah. I don't get what that has to do with anything?"

She reached under her chair and pulled out a cookie tin. Opening it with practiced ease, she offered me a gingersnap. I plucked one from the tin and took a nibble. The sweet heat of ginger and spices hit my tongue.

"My mother made these at Christmas time every year." She sighed as she examined her own cookie. "Every year she would take me through the baking process and every year I burned the shit out of every pan I put in the oven. No matter what I did or how careful I was those motherfucking cookies would not turn out right." I chuckled at the profanity as I ate my treat. "Twenty years I struggled. I cannot *tell* you how many poor gingersnaps met an unkind death at my hands. Pissed me off because my sister sure could make snaps! I felt like I was letting down my mother with my inability to bake a good snap like her and my sister. I told her that one year and she tweaked my nose and told me to stop being foolish. She said that her pride in me did not come from cookie-baking, it came from the fact that I was a good human being. I bet your father and mother feel the same."

I had some trouble swallowing for a second. "Thanks," I whispered and took another cookie. "I had a dream last night…"

. . .

THE DAY AFTER MY FIRST SESSION I CALLED WORK AND informed them that I was taking a leave of absence for mental health reasons. I knew that Adam could be on campus because he'd easily met his bail, and being where we'd interacted on a regular basis freaked me out. Like, to the point that even thinking of stepping foot on campus apart from seeing my therapist threw me into a panic attack. I had never had panic attacks, but the morning after that initial consult with Dr. Morgan, I did. A pretty severe one with chills and nausea. Ryker talked me through it, but suggested strongly that I do some heavy therapy for a while. And so I did. Doc Morgan wiggled me into her schedule daily for three weeks.

Those were some really killer sessions. She walked me through so much, deep shit that made me rage then cry like an infant. When the sexual stuff got too hard, we'd switch up and talk about my strengths. At this point I felt as if I had none, and told her so, but she insisted I do some thinking. Ryker helped with that assignment, extolling all my amazing qualities then insisting I write them down and take them back the next day.

As I read over his list, there were a few that I could agree with. I was loyal, had a good work ethic, and I was loving. He thought I was intelligent. That I scoffed at. Doc Morgan had asked me why I felt that I was dumb, my words, not hers.

"Smart people don't allow themselves to be used like that."

"Ah," she had said. "So women who are raped and assaulted are stupid for being in that situation?"

"*No!* No, shit, no. I'm not blaming the victim, hell no!" I quickly countered.

"It sounds to me like you are. You're blaming yourself for something an evil person did to you. Do you think that you're better than a female victim?"

"No, God, stop!" I had barked, springing from my chair to glower down at her. "Stop making me sound like a dick! I would never blame a woman for something some filthy jerk did to her!"

"Then why don't you extend that same compassion to yourself?"

That took all the wind out of my sails. I fell back into the chair, blinking dully at her. "I don't know. Because I'm a man."

We somehow managed to get through that hour, but the next wasn't much easier. None of them were. There were so many things, new things, that I was feeling. The loss of control was overwhelming at times. The fear of seeing Adam somewhere kept me on edge. We worked on something she called "cognitive processing" which was fancy psych talk for working on self-deprecating patterns and triggers. She had me wear a rubber band around my wrist. I felt stupid, but one night at dinner, about eighteen days into my altered life, Ryker and I had gone out to eat at a local Mexican restaurant.

I was fine, not great, still edgy but okay. Then a waiter walked by with a pitcher of what looked to be Sea Breezes. Just like that, I was back on that patio, grabbing at the table, trying to not faceplant. I snapped that rubber band as hard as I could to help identify the trigger. It was one of what would probably be many things that might set off a memory, but at least I could recognize it as that.

I'd been raised to think that talking to a mental health provider was a sign of weakness. Real men didn't sit on a couch and talk about their problems. They buried them and carried on. I was not the same man I had been, and while I would always hate Adam for what he'd done to me, at least now I was learning that talking to your partner or your therapist *was* something real men did.

Communication was the only thing that was going to get me through this. Thank God Ryker liked to talk because we sure were doing a lot of it now. With two weeks to go until the big day, we spent all of our time together expressing all of our feelings, withholding nothing now. It felt wonderful. Freeing. Liberating. Which was why I'd asked him to come to my next session. He readily agreed. And I felt even deeper in love with him, if that were even possible.

10

RYKER

JACOB AND I HAD BEEN SEEING THE COUNSELOR FOR THREE weeks now, and what we'd discovered in our chats with Dr. Morgan made us love each other more—if that was even possible. Still, the full and frank discussions we were having meant I was slowly becoming more paranoid with every passing day. I was sure he wanted to marry me—that was never in question, but whether our life goals were the same was becoming more the issue. He'd talked last night about leaving Tucson completely. Not in a specific I've-booked-a-U-Haul-and-I'm-heading-for-Alaska kind of way, but in a general, maybe-Tucson-isn't-the-best-place-for-me way. I knew what he was implying —that he was hemmed in, that he didn't need heat and desert, but farms and animals and *something else.* But, I had hockey, and that hockey was in Tucson, and we needed to find a compromise.

We were two parts of the same person, and *needed* each other, and the rest of our lives started with finding a common purpose. Counseling had gotten us so far, but everything I saw in Jacob screamed a need to get out of the city and away from the college and the memories of what had happened. It didn't help that the media were all over the case like white on rice, with Adam's name rising to the surface despite the best efforts of his legal team, and that Adam's name was being linked to unspecified issues. He'd pulled out of working with the college, magnanimously leaving his funding in place after making a simple statement about conflict of interest.

But we still had to go through the crap of meetings between our lawyers and his lawyers, and the cops, and the feds, and God knows who else. At least today's meeting, our lawyers against Adam's lawyers, was being held on neutral ground. I hated when anyone came to our home and disrupted the harmony we were working so hard on.

Maybe sitting in Jacob's truck watching cat videos until we were due in the offices was a good time to talk about a compromise for our future, and I had some theories and ideas that I wanted to run by him. I'd been sitting on this information for a while, considering whether it was helpful or not to talk about a long distance relationship so that Jacob could be *happy*.

"So I talked to Eric Dobson. Remember him?"

Jacob shot me a thoughtful glance. "Eric? Isn't he the one from your private school, the one with the Lamborghini?"

Trust Jacob to zero in on the car—he loved cars and it was what he did, and just another quirk that made me love him more. "Yep, he's a genius with a baseball bat, drafted to New Orleans like his dad, blah blah, met a

Canadian girl, Anita, who was working down in the Big Easy for a year."

"So, Eric, what about him?" Jacob prompted when I paused a little too long.

"He's doing good. I mean, he fell madly in love with Anita, and when she went back to Quebec for work they made it work, spending their time commuting to meet up when they can off-season, around her work. I'm just thinking, what if we invest in some land in Minnesota, a farm where you live, and I get to you when I can, and you come visit when you can. I could rent a room from Alex when I'm in Tucson, or something. Plenty of married couples live apart for a few years and make it work."

"I see where this is going." Jacob turned in his seat to face me. "You're saying that we get married, and then I live on a farm in another state where you imagine I'll be happy, and you play hockey and you think you'll be happy, and we see each other in the summer and maybe the odd weekday?" His tone was even, but I saw his eye twitch and he was tense.

"It's possible." I watched his expression closely, but couldn't tell if he thought I was an idiot or not. I'd been thinking through every option to get to a point where Jacob was happy because even though he was still working at the college, something fundamental had snapped inside him after the Adam *thing*. He was restless, angry, couldn't focus on data when all he wanted was to be outside with physical work, and I could see pain in his expression when he thought I wasn't looking. Counseling was doing something, but it wasn't going to fix *everything*.

He closed his eyes and shook his head. "Being apart isn't right for us, Ry. I couldn't do it."

"Okay, then I could retire after my current contract is done, coach somewhere, bank the money. If we got a place with a pond like your parents' farm, then in the winter we could skate and—"

"Don't be ridiculous," Jacob laughed, and that hurt, and he must have seen that in my face because he instantly stopped, then took my hand tightly. "I'm sorry, I didn't mean... look, it's like this. You were made to play hockey, you're a genius, it's your career, and it makes you the person I fell in love with. So, let's not talk about that, okay?"

"Okay, so next option is that I don't retire but maybe we move away from the city and closer to somewhere where there's wide open spaces."

"No, I love you for all of this Ry, but you wouldn't even be saying that if I hadn't gotten involved with the Bygenta project."

"I would. Because I love you, and I know your heart is with the farm and the animals, and nature. That is part of you," I began to throw his own words back at him, and he smiled. "It makes you the person I fell in love with."

"Let's leave the talking for now," he said, and cradled my cheek.

I smiled back at him, and leaned in for a kiss, managing a brief peck before the alarm on the phone reminded us we needed to go in. With reluctance, we left the truck and headed into the plush whisper-quiet officers of Lesser, Movvern, and Bligh, lawyers for the

Raptors, and home to what I could only imagine were *many* hockey secrets.

I guessed they must have been used to everything from trades to Colorado-gets-a-baby type incidents, but being so invested in the fiancé of one of their players was probably a new one. We were here today because Adam's lawyers had called for a private meeting, and I had this sickening feeling about where this was going. Money. Bribery. It was inevitable that at some point Adam would want to try to make all of this go away, although what he thought he would get out of paying Jacob off, when there was evidence of other acts he'd carried out on his computers, I don't know.

Adam's lawyers looked confident, all wide smiles and handshaking, but I could see their calculating glances as they looked Jacob up and down, and I knew them for the sharks they were. They spent close to fifteen minutes extolling the virtues of Adam Isaksson, summarizing the situation from their side, and our lawyers let them. They talked about Jacob's previous drinking issues, had photos from my Instagram from last New Year, talked about finances, and doubt, and evidence, and cast aspersions on Jacob's usefulness as a witness given his *lifestyle*. What they didn't do was admit Adam had plied Jacob with drugged alcohol, but they did show a static video of Jacob half on and half off a sofa, pointing out that Adam didn't approach Jacob until the moment he began to wake up and that it was to *help him*. There was no volume of the video, and all I could do was grasp Jacob's hand as I watched. According to time stamps, Jacob had been unconscious for only ninety-three minutes, and they admitted to the use of drugs but called it recreational and agreed upon. I called bullshit on the time frame, and as to the rest? I had to bite my tongue and stay quiet as our team had encouraged us to do.

"With his solid reputation of philanthropy, and his charitable donations, Mr. Isaksson is a force to be reckoned with," they summarized and I tensed. Was that a threat? Before I could say anything though, the opposing lawyer carried on with a silky smooth tone. "All of this should be enough for you to look upon our client kindly," Adam's lawyer concluded to Jacob in a condescending tone. "In addition, to recompense you for undue hurt or discomfort, I'm authorized to offer you a settlement figure of ten million dollars, in exchange for you signing a full non-disclosure—"

"No." Jacob was final, his tone clipped.

"We can add a further three million as a charitable donation to—"

"No."

"Mr. Benson—"

Jacob stood so suddenly his chair hit the wall, and startled everyone. Except me—I knew exactly what he was going to do, and I couldn't have been prouder of him.

"I said no. I don't want money, I want to stop Adam Isaksson doing the same thing to someone *smaller*, and *more vulnerable than* me, someone who might have died. In summary, no."

I glanced at our side of the table, at the wide-eyed but approving Raptors' lawyers, and followed Jacob out, bypassing the elevator and heading down the fire exit stairs. We made it down five flights and out to the street in total silence, then I followed him past a coffee shop and a car rental place, and he took a left down an alley then stopped near a dumpster.

Only after he reached this private space did the air leave him in a *whoosh* and he bent over and rested his hands on his knees.

"Shit. Fuck," he muttered.

I rubbed his broad back. I would be there for him no matter what he did, or said. Hell, right about now, I'd probably have held his coat while he dug a hole to bury Adam in.

"Everything is okay," I said as I continued touching him, all while hoping it helped.

"Shit, Ry, what have I done to you?" he said after a while, and then used the wall to steady himself as he straightened.

"What? You haven't done anything to me."

Jacob shook his head and backed away just a little when I reached for his hand. "If I take this all the way, if I appear in court, people will know. They'll look at us and they'll wonder how someone like me could have let myself get into that situation. We already get shit for being together, for our *unconventional* relationship." I winced at the latest thing that had been said about us in an article on Colorado and his recent investment in an emu sanctuary outside of Sedona. Fuck the bigots and their comments on our *lifestyle*.

"We ignore them—"

"Who will believe that anyone could hurt me? Look at me, whatever the doc says, I'm a big guy, and I let myself get into that situation. I can't shake the feeling that I could have stopped—"

"Jacob, you need to stop saying this shit. I don't care what people think. I don't have any room in my soul for the people who would say shit. Or the ones who use stereotypes to frame their bigoted world views. This is about *us*, and we're okay." I stepped closer, and this time he didn't move away, and he let me take his hand. I called that a win.

He was wide-eyed though, and on the edge of panicking. "The Raptors will trade you. This will get blown out of proportion, and all you have to do is have a run of bad games and management will look at this as the reason why."

"Firstly, the management will do the best for the team. The only reason they'll trade me is if I let this affect my playing, and I'm determined it won't. Secondly, if I get traded then maybe I get to play in Canada, or Minnesota, or hell, anywhere with farms and animals and snow. Whatever happens we'll be together."

"I love you," Jacob murmured, and tugged me into a close hug.

"I love you, too," I said, and kissed his neck before tucking my chin against his shoulder. "We'll be okay, we'll fight whatever needs fighting, and on Valentine's Day we'll get married, everything will be fine."

He tensed and then sighed. "You know what *will* happen, right?"

"Hmm? What?"

"You'll get traded to freaking Florida."

11

JACOB

THE FAMILIES ARRIVED JUST BEFORE VALENTINE'S DAY, ready for the wedding. My folks on an early flight and Ten, Jared, and their new baby on a later one. Four hours after that, Ryker's mom and her second family flew into Tucson International. There was no time now to dwell on the whole lost hours crap. I was determined to not let it interfere with our beautiful hearts and flowers wedding in any way. This marriage was the one stable thing in my existence right now. My job—hell, my entire *life*—was in the air.

To be honest, I wasn't sure I even wanted to do research anymore as the fantasy about a small farm with cattle and horses was taking root in my heart. We went to eat at a local Italian restaurant for dinner. The interior was decorated with pink and red hearts and a poster on the main door advertised a Valentine's event which made our wedding in two days seem so real. I made small talk, smiled at my mom and dad, joked with Ten, and kissed

Ryker whenever I could. But while that was all rolling along on the outside, on the inside I was still in that pit.

"... to see this desert camp of Colorado's," Mom was saying.

I smiled at her across my plate of manicotti, Ryker's thigh tight to mine. He'd been at my side for days now, and it was his support that had gotten me through everything.

"It's amazing!" Ry said, giving me a soft smile then extolling the camp as if it were Buckingham Palace. The meal finally ended and we ran my folks to their hotel where all of our families were staying.

Mom pulled me to the side after we escorted them into the lobby. Dad and Ry went to find some deodorant at the corner store; Dad had forgotten to pack his. Ten, Jared, and baby Charlotte had to get ready for bed and a bottle, and Ryker's sisters were itching to watch a movie in their room so his mom and step-dad said goodnight after a long ass day.

"You look peaked. Are you feeling okay?"

"Yep, fine. Nervous. Work stuff." I fluffed her off but knew it wouldn't last. She had a sense about her only child. I'd never been able to hide anything from her for long. "I'm thinking of possibly switching fields."

"Oh."

"Yeah," I shoved my hands into the front pocket of my jeans. "Research isn't working out. I might ask for a transfer into something more hands on, or even look for a ranch job."

"Oh."

"So yeah, just wedding jitters and job junk." I flashed her a smile.

She stared at me from under knitted eyebrows doing her perceptive-mom thing which freaked me out a little. Thank god that Dad and Ryker showed up, with deodorant and a bag of spicy corn chips, which broke the standoff, and we waved at my parents as they left to go to their room. Only, Mom's gaze never left me.

"Christ," I huffed and made a beeline for my truck. Ryker jogged up and stood beside me.

"You should tell them, Jacob." I shook my head vehemently. "They'd want to know."

"Nope, they wouldn't. Dad would never be able to look at me as a man again. He had enough trouble with me being gay, Ryker!"

"Okay, okay, don't get upset. I'm not trying to piss you off, but I think our parents need to know." I paused by the front bumper, terror gripping my bowels. Ryker ran around me and looked up into my face. There was so much worry in his gaze, and I'd been the one to put it there. If only I would have listened to him… "Babe." He took one of my fisted hands, and peeled the fingers open then slid his between them. "Look at it this way. Say we have a son or daughter someday and something like this happens to him or her." I felt sick at the thought but saw right where he was going. "We'd want to be there for them as they struggled through a really difficult time, right?"

I looked skyward. Then slowly, painfully, bobbed my head. Telling my father was going to kill me, I knew it. But, again, Ryker was right. They deserved to know. I would want to know. And so, after a moment or ten, I turned and walked back into the hotel, clutching Ryker's hand for dear life. We were silent on the ride up to the fifth floor where we'd gotten the families rooms. My feet felt like they were cinderblocks. My heart was skipping, the manicotti I'd eaten was now sitting badly.

"We got this," Ryker kept whispering, hand in mine, until we stood outside room 518.

It took me a long time to work up the courage to knock. Mom opened the door a moment later, a smile on her face that faded when I opened my mouth to speak but nothing came out.

"We have something to tell you," Ryker murmured. "Something... unpleasant."

"I knew it. I *knew* something was wrong," Mom whispered as fear settled on her face. A face that looked far older than she was. A face lined by a life of worry and debt. Most of that worry a direct result of the gay son who couldn't keep the family farm from sinking. I sucked. I was stupid. "Are you two calling off the wedding? Breaking up?"

"No!" I burst out, shaken at how loud I'd been. "No, nothing like that. I love Ryker so much I can't even—" I stopped to gather myself. "Can we come inside? This isn't a hallway discussion."

Mom stepped back, pale and shaken, and we walked into the suite to find my father sitting on the short brown sofa, shoes off, staring at us. Obviously, he'd heard the discussion in the doorway. Ryker released my hand and I sat on the creaky rolling chair by the desk. Mom sat beside Dad, wringing her hands. I tried several times to speak but the words were jammed up inside me like ice on a thawing river. My shoulders dropped and my head bowed, my gaze on my hands dangling between my legs.

Ryker knelt beside me, one arm on my thigh, the other taking one of my chilly hands. "There was this guy that Jacob worked with and he… well, he did some stuff."

"Ry, let me," I finally coughed out, lifting my sight from the carpet to my parents. "Adam. His name is Adam." Mom and Dad listened as I wound my way through the story. When I stopped, years later by the feels, at where things stood now, Mom was weeping and my father's face was set in stone.

"Oh, baby," Mom coughed, leaving the sofa to take me into her arms. I slid an arm around her waist, burying my face into her breast as I had as a young boy with a scraped knee. "I knew you were haunted by something. This bastard is going to pay for hurting you!"

That made me smile. Mothers. Oh my God, they were the fiercest creatures when their young had been hurt. I sniffled, keeping the tears at bay, and pulled away. She kissed my forehead then had to move aside for my father. I glanced away, sure he was stepping into my space to tell me what a miserable excuse of a man and son I was.

"I get first crack at this son of a bitch," Dad growled then pulled me up to my feet and hugged me close. I held my father tight. "No one hurts my boy."

"Thank you for still loving me, Dad," I sputtered. Soon there were four in on the hug and I felt safe in that small circle. Safe and so very loved. And ready to marry the man who was smushed in the middle of the hugs and tears.

12

RYKER

When we left Jacob's parents' room I could tell that Jacob was exhausted but there was one more visit I wanted to make and I tugged him to stop just at the elevators.

"Could we quickly see Dad?" I asked softly, and I didn't have to add anything else because unspoken was the rest —that I wanted to tell Dad about what had happened before any news filtered out from the Raptors and made its way around the NHL at the speed of light. So far the lawyers on both sides had kept a lid on everything that connected Jacob, from our side it was to protect him, from the other side I assume it was to keep Jacob's experience from taking a hold on the public conscience. We hadn't played the Railers since that last road trip, and I'd kept our weekly calls generic, slipping more into texting, and citing that Jacob and I were busy with the wedding. Dad never called me out on it, and I get the feeling he thought maybe Jacob and I were still having issues, but I didn't correct him and none of it was sitting right with me.

"Of course," Jacob said after a short pause.

"You don't have to… I mean I could go up and—"

"No, together." He held my hand, kissed me hard, and then hugged me. I knocked on the door as quietly as I could, aware that Lottie might be asleep, and when the door opened the first thing Dad did was press a finger to his lips and gesture over his shoulder. Ten was lying on the sofa, Lottie on his chest, both of them dead to the world. I'd never seen anything so heartachingly sweet as my little sister asleep in Ten's arms.

"We could get money for that," I whispered. "Send it to the hordes at Ten-Watch." He made a banner shape in the air. "Hockey phenom Tennant Rowe and baby daughter."

"I reckon millions of fans would spontaneously explode," Jacob whispered back.

Dad ushered us into the separate sitting room, and then hugging me as if he hadn't seen me in years. I couldn't help sinking into his hug, because it might not have been years, but it *had* been months. He hugged Jacob as well, and my heart, already overflowing with love seeing Ten and Lottie, swelled some more.

"Sit down, boys," he gestured to the sofa and took the single chair. "Tell me what's going on." That was my dad, always going straight to the point, and weirdly enough I felt defensive just as I had in my teenage years when he'd seen right through me. I couldn't channel teenage-Ryker and say there was nothing wrong, because there was so much that was wrong. "Is it the wedding? Are you two okay? Whatever is wrong we can fix this, because you two belong together. Oh god, are you ill? Is one of you ill?"

My teenage angst slid away, and abruptly my dad was back there, unsure of what was going on and frightened for me and Jacob.

Jacob gripped my hand, "No, sir, we're okay. Only, I worked for a man called Adam Isaksson."

"I know—he's the rich tech guy with the seeds, right?"

"Yeah," Jacob paused. Then the story fell out of him, and only when I heard a sharp inhalation from the doorway did I realize that Ten had woken up, Lottie still asleep in his arms, and had heard most of the story.

"I'm sorry, I didn't mean to interrupt, I needed to get..." He picked up the travel cot to leave.

"Stay, Ten. Please," Jacob murmured.

"Hang on." Ten went into the other room, laid Lottie in the cot and then came back to sit on the side of Dad's chair. "Do you need lawyers, we can get lawyers."

"The Raptors have our back," I said quickly.

"Then how can we help?" Ten blurted. "We have to be able to do something. What a fucking asshole, what a... shit... fuck... Jesus." That was about all Ten could manage before in a flurry of movement he pulled Jacob to stand and hugged him hard. "That fucking fucker, I'm so fucking sorry."

"I'm okay, we're okay," Jacob said firmly.

He hugged Ten, though, and when they separated emotion glittered in Ten's eyes. "We're taking him down."

"No," Jacob said in the simplest of terms. "Your reputation and career could be at stake Ten. Not to mention Ryker's and Jared's, I'm going to do this myself."

Well, that was news to me, and I stiffened and then stood and shoved Jacob. Just a little, but enough to know I was there in front of him when he wouldn't look at me.

"We're doing this together. Me and you."

"And me," Ten announced, "I know people who know people, I'll call Stan—"

"Ten, sit down." Dad grabbed Ten and yanked him to sit. "No one is calling Stan, or hiring *people*. Jacob, Ryker, sit down." When we'd all sat down we waited for Dad's words of wisdom. "You're family, Jacob, and you have been since the moment my son met you. I love you like another son, and anyone who hurts you is on my shit list. Ten and I will be by your side through every step of this, if you need us we'll be there, if you want us to stand aside, we will. But through all of it, you can count on our unwavering support and love."

"Yep," Ten agreed. "Always."

"Dad…" My voice broke from the flood of emotion welling inside of me. Maybe I needed my dad to tell me that he was there to look after me and Jacob. Maybe it was knowing that they were in our corner, whatever it was, I was done, and I hugged Jacob so hard and never wanted to leave his hold. "I love you, Dad, and you, Ten."

"Of course you do, *son*," Ten smirked to lighten the charged room. "We're awesome parents." Dad elbowed Ten who grunted theatrically. "One thing though," he paused and tapped his lip. "Don't think for one second that any of this means we'll go easy on the Raptors in March."

Jacob snorted a laugh, and we all heard Lottie do this

kind of yelp thing. I went to collect her, Ten made a bottle, Jared changed her diaper, and Jacob fed her.

What with this and Jacob's parents' reactions, we were blessed. We had family in our corner, and that was all that mattered.

OUR LAWYER KEPT TALKING.

"Arizona sentencing laws make the prison term dependent on several factors such as the age of the victim or the criminal record of the offender…" The words meant nothing to me. They were just that, words, a long list of reasons why Adam had entered into some kind of arrangement with the prosecutor.

"Wait," Jacob interrupted. "So Adam pleads guilty to this lesser charge in exchange for a more lenient sentence? Or is he looking to get charges dropped?"

"Not at all. He's giving up the right to a potentially vindicating not-guilty verdict, by accepting the guilt for your attack, and pleading out on the videos on his computer."

"I don't get it, is there going to be a trial?" I asked, when Jacob frowned at me.

"Basically a guilty or no-contest plea is entered as a judge-approved plea-bargain—"

"No, in English," Jacob interrupted.

"The deal is eight years, a criminal conviction which will show on the defendant's criminal record, and mandatory inclusion on the sex offenders list."

"And this is for real?" I asked as Jacob slumped back on the sofa.

If this was right, then there would be no court case, no public opinion on the situation, Jacob's name might not even be included. Was this the best thing to happen? Or was this absolutely the wrong thing? Did Jacob want his day in court?

"Subsequent media coverage could cause the judge to rethink the plea bargain, but for now, the situation we find ourselves in is that it is in the best interest of several government departments that this is dealt with as privately as possible. The defendant has several high-level connections and this has come down from them, which leaves us with a rather difficult decision."

"And that is?"

"Our advice to you is that we accept the eight years, and the fact Adam Isaksson will face financial ruination, and a criminal record."

"We'll need time to think," I murmured, but Jacob shook his head.

"I agree," he said firmly, and stared at me as he said the words.

"We will courier papers to you for signature, and you have our contact details, please stay in touch, Jacob."

As soon as the call ended Jacob deflated and sunk back in the sofa.

"Are you sure?" I said, and sat next to him, resting my head on his chest.

"Completely. I'm one of many, and some will have no knowledge of this, or will have lived with this for so long that it's become a memory for them. I want to save the entire fucking world, but t's not on me to do anything else apart from look after us. I want to do *something*, reach out to anyone who needs help, but do we need court? Going up against his money, and pulling everyone into the hell of proceedings. I need to finish this, Ry, I need this part to be done."

"Then it will be."

We sat there for the longest time, just holding each other, and whispering promises of what our lives would be like, and slowly shock gave way to grief and then acceptance.

But through all of the emotions we were there together, and that was what mattered.

13

JACOB

THE DAY OF THE WEDDING WAS HOT, BRIGHT, AND FULL OF love, and I glanced to the right and there stood Ryker.

His suit was perfectly cut and fitted, the color bringing out the soft hues in his eyes. He was trying his best to fight back some serious laughter. Hands clasped, we waited while Colorado, in full, flamboyant Colorado stage gear of tattered jeans, long flowing heart covered kimono, and bare feet, strolled the aisle we'd just walked down, singing Aerosmith's 'Amazing' while strumming an old guitar.

"I thought we were going with something by Dwight Yoakum," I whispered to the side.

"Colorado said he couldn't sing country and western for some reason. Still want to marry me?" Ryker asked as the strolling tattooed minstrel reached the end of his hard rock serenade, bowed deeply then kissed the officiant.

"It'll take more than an old Aerosmith song to put me off," I replied, squeezing his fingers then releasing them so I could clap.

A few flowers were tossed at the rocker's feet. He gathered them up, kissed us both on the mouth, and then strutted back to Joe and Maddie in the second row of chairs. The interior of this marquee was themed in red and pink, and what appeared to be a million tiny white lights twisted in and among hearts and flowers, Apollo wasn't joking that it was obvious that getting married on Valentine's Day meant that the decorating concept had to match. Voile filtered the lights, and the whole effect was stunning.

Once Pastor Gena from the United Church of Assembled Love—a non-denominational church that fully welcomed LGBTQ people—shook off the surprise of being kissed by Colorado, she looked out over the assembled, a small group of our family and closest friends plus the teammates, new and old, that had arrived.

Benoit, Ethan, Scott, and Hayne had flown out to join us. Ryker's folks and mine were in the front row, all the parents were teary-eyed. All the Raptors grinning, even Coach Carmichael, who was kind of stiff at times. All the kids were antsy already, with two grumpy babies rounding out the afternoon gathering.

It was a simple affair, small yet perfect with the glory of the desert visible through the open parts of the marquee. Our vows were short but deeply felt pledges to love each other through all the good and bad times. Never were words more heartfelt than those troths, for Ryker and I had already weathered some horrid things and yet, here we were, committing ourselves to each other in spite of the beating that life had given us. If that didn't bode well for a new marriage, I didn't know what did.

After the I-dos and the bird seed shower, we cleared away the chairs and set up for the buffet. Apollo and his aunt had cooked for days, and as the food was brought out, pan after pan, we took pictures away from the camp, using the cacti and the sand as background. The DJ that Apollo had lined up began to play a wild blend of country and western, rock, and oldies. There was no tight schedule to stick to, pretty much we just played it by ear until the first dance was ready to commence. I guess one didn't monkey with the dances. I'd been sipping champagne and talking to Alex and Seb, who were planning their own wedding celebration in England over the summer break, when my new husband came up beside me.

"It's time for our dance," Ryker said and took my hand.

I passed my glass of bubbly to Seb and followed Ryker to the makeshift dance floor the DJ had supplied. The small group fell quiet when we faced each other, Ryker's body brushing mine, as we started to move to "And I Love Him," a reimagined Beatles song performed by Benjamin Gifford. His hand fit perfectly in mine as we swayed back and forth. I wasn't much of a dancer but he led me without it being obvious. I leaned down to rub my cheek against his.

"You're my life," I whispered beside his ear.

He turned his head to steal a kiss before dropping his head to my shoulder. "Happy Valentine's Day," he murmured.

"Back at ya," I kissed him again, and then the dance ended with wild applause. We then broke apart and went to find our moms.

I danced with my mother to "Mama's Song" by Carrie Underwood. She cried.

"Are those happy tears?" I asked and got a wobbly nod.

"Yes, so happy." She coughed then rested her wet cheek to my chest.

Ryker danced with his mother to "Mother Like Mine" by The Band Perry. She cried too. I hoped they were happy tears like my mother's tears had been. Then, the music took an upbeat and the dance floor filled with hockey players and their dates.

Ryker and I mingled, trying to be good hosts. We visited with family members at the tables, sitting with Ryker's new sister, Lottie, so Ten and Jared could have a slow dance. Ryker looked incredible with a baby in his arms, and the yearning for a simpler life grew that much stronger.

The day sped by, and I found myself laughing now and again at the team or the family's antics. Night settled over the camp, and with it the last of the guests were heading out. I shook hands with Ten, got hugged, and kissed on the cheek by Jared, and had my face smothered with kisses from my mom. Dad hugged me and told me he was proud. I nearly broke down but held it together.

"Okay, so the food is in the fridge in plastic containers. You two won't have to leave this camp for a week!" Apollo winked then bussed our cheeks.

"Thank you so much," Ryker said as Henry waited in the darkness for his man. "You really have no idea how much this all means to us."

"He's right." I clapped Apollo on the shoulder. "It's

been... well, it's been a rough few months, but this wedding was perfect."

Apollo bowed with flair. "I am *so* good at parties! I should open a business." A horn honked. "Ah! That's my honey man. You two enjoy this week. Heal from whatever darkness has fallen over you in each other's arms."

Off he skipped, and then it was just Ryker and me. I turned to face him. He was tired but happy. Cradling his face between my hands, I kissed him, softly but with all the passion I held within me.

"You're my strength," I whispered over his lips. He carded his hands into my hair and rose to his toes for another taste. "I want to do this right... the wedding night but..."

"Shh, let's just follow our hearts."

And so we did. We slipped into the camp, closed the doors, and made our way to the big bed in the master bedroom. With the windows open and the moon falling over us in wide, white strips, we crawled into bed after our clothes were shed.

"My heart is yours, always," I confessed as we lay beside each other. His touch made me shiver but I moved closer, seeking something that only Ryker could give me. We rocked as one, just touching and kissing, the passion rising slowly just as the moon in the window had.

"I was scared that after the thing with Adam this might not ever come back," I confessed as I ran a hand over his hip, my body responding to him with a natural ease that my brain had feared forever lost. We'd not touched like this since before that terrible night...

"Don't push it, okay?" He leaned up on one arm to study me lying under him.

A coyote howled far off in the distance, then a yip followed the plaintive wail.

"You hear that? I bet they're mates looking for each other." I brushed some wayward curls from his face, the moon painting his skin milky white. "They're fated, just like you and me. I'm not pushing anything, babe. You and me, married, loving each other is what I need right now. Love me a bit more, Ry."

"Fuck, but you're my whole world," he replied heatedly. His body was hard, sliding over mine, he nipped along my jaw as he took us both in hand.

I clung to him, let him lead me, lead *us*, to a sweet, tender place where we tumbled over each other into an explosion of joy and release that robbed me of breath and words.

"God, that was…" Ryker panted, spread out over me, his weight familiar and cherished.

"It was." I kissed his bouncy curls. "You made it that way. Special. You knew what I needed. You always know. I just… I am so glad you're here in my life. I love you."

We lay there with each other, arms and legs knotted, his head on my chest, the night air growing cooler as it crept through the window. Neither of us wanted to rise but we had a bit of a mess to clean up. He and I showered together, kissing and soaping, falling more in love with the other as the water sluiced over us. I worked shampoo into his thick hair, marveling at the texture and bounce. I'd been sure this night would be a disaster but Ryker had made it easy and free, which was so Ryker it made me chuckle to myself.

"What?" he asked over a wet shoulder.

I massaged his scalp then kissed the nape of his neck, uncaring about the bubbles streaming over his skin.

"I was freaking out about taking you to bed, you know. It's been... I've been weird about sex since... that night and Adam."

"Yeah no mentioning his name during our honeymoon."

"Right sorry. That night with the monster."

"Better." He turned to look at me, his hair thick with mango-scented bubbles. "And there is no wrong or right way to do a wedding night. Making love doesn't always have to be about penetrative sex, right? Neither one of us has to prove our virginity or anything. We came together as a loving couple, that's all the consummation that we need. Fuck that stupid ass archaic shit anyway. What is that all about? Do asexual people's marriages not count because someone didn't stick a dick into someone else?"

His passion made me smile. "I think it's still required legally, babe."

"Well fuck that. It's an outdated belief. Like just because you sleep with someone you'll be with them forever? Pfft. Right. Just check the divorce rates. All the consummation we need is the vows that we made to love one another and spend our lives together. Anyway, who can prove what we did and didn't do? They going to send in royal watchers?"

"I'm not arguing with you, I was just—"

He rose to his toes. "Stop worrying. Everything we do

in bed I love. Now, rinse me out so we can go raid the fridge. I'm dying to have another helping of that black bean dish Maria made."

"If you eat more beans I'll make you sleep with the coyotes," I said as I gently spun him to face the pulsating water.

"Would you really?"

"Eat more beans and see."

He did. I didn't kick him out to sleep with the coyotes, but I sure wanted to.

THE NEXT COUPLE OF DAYS WERE ABSOLUTE HEAVEN. BY the end of our first day at camp I had fallen deeply in love with the desert. Ryker and I had spent our time out and about, only allowing ourselves an hour of social media. Ry, being the IG hound that he was, made massive photo dumps to his IG account in that hour. Images of him and me star-gazing and sand-surfing, sitting around fires at camp, lounging in the hot tub, riding the dunes in Colorado's dune buggy, and spotting wildlife, collecting all the paper hearts that had decorated the cabin. Our hours were soft, tender things, full of whispers and touches, where there was no pressure to do anything that didn't feel right yet.

The second morning of our getaway, my phone buzzed at six sharp. Rolling over Ryker to find it, I slapped a hand to the nightstand, knocked the bottle of lube to the floor, mumbled, and finally located my phone. I squinted at the name on the caller ID then frowned. Ryker groaned. I moved off his back and he drifted back to sleep. I let the call go to my voicemail as I slipped out of bed. I pulled the covers over Ryker's naked backside, stepped into a pair of clean jeans and a tee, and padded out to the kitchen to make coffee. As it perked, I listened to the voice mail from the university. It was pretty much as I had expected.

They were giving me two options. I could return to the campus and pick up where I'd left off before I'd taken a sabbatical. Or they would give me a settlement dependent on legal documents for me to sign in which I would declare I didn't hold the university liable. Of course I didn't blame the University, because they didn't know Adam any more than me, but I wanted to make sure it never happened again. I eyed the settlement sum with wide eyes. It was generous. *Extremely* generous. In all of it they made sure to confirm that robust systems would be further strengthened to support anyone going through what I had.

While Ryker slept off our late night of star-gazing and mutual hand jobs, I found my sneakers, checked them for scorpions, and then slid my feet into them. With nothing but a thermos of coffee, a worn Raptors T-shirt, jeans, and sneakers sans socks, I left the camp for a rise about half a mile away. It looked out over a vast area of sand and desert grasslands. Down below a group of prairie dogs were waking up, entertaining me as I pondered my future. I glanced out over cacti and sage grass; various insects were stirring as were songbirds. The sky was mottled red and yellow, and far away the mountains kissed the rising sun.

"Hey," Ryker called as he came up behind me. "I woke up and you were gone."

"Mm, I wanted to commune with the desert. I got a call from the university." I pulled out my phone and let him listen to the dean's message. His mouth fell open when he heard the settlement sum.

"That is a *lot* of zeroes," he said as he passed the cell back. I nodded, took a sip of coffee from the thermos then offered it to him. He took it and sipped a bit. "What will you do?"

"I'm not sure I can go back to campus. It'll be a constant reminder. I'm not sure I even want to go back to research at all."

"What do you want to do?" he asked then passed the thermos back. A small green snake slithered slowly past, looking for a sunny rock to warm itself on. We let him pass.

"Did you know that Colorado owns close to five hundred acres?" I glanced to my right. His hair was sleep-tousled yet and he had a tiny love bite on his neck.

"No. How do you know that?" He folded his legs into a lotus as a bird trilled from the top of a tall cactus.

"I asked him at the reception. Five hundred acres and he uses maybe two."

"And that's important, why?"

"I was thinking that if I took the Uni settlement, it doesn't change the legal path against Adam. But with the money we could buy a few hundred acres and get some horses. Build a house, a barn, maybe set up some sort of rehab center for LGBT teens that have been sexually assaulted." I had to pause and let my heart slow. *Sexually assaulted.* I'd never used that term before. I'd always called what Adam had done to me something else. Doctor Morgan would've been be so proud. "They could come out to the ranch, work with the horses and other livestock, get some counseling." I shrugged. "I don't know. I think it would work. I looked up this other place online, it's in Texas. I sent them an email to enquire about setup and shit." I peeked over at him staring at the prairie dogs down below. "What do you think?"

"I think if it's what you want to do then do it," he replied thoughtfully.

"No, it's not just my call, Ry. We're married now. One person doesn't make all the calls, especially on something this big. If we do this, build the ranch, you'll have to live there with me. Are you cool with teenagers hanging around, and the issues that some of them may bring to our home?"

He spun on his ass to face me. "Jacob, I am totally fine with the idea." I raised an eyebrow. "Totally. Fine. Will there be some adjustment? Yeah, sure, but we'll adjust. I can see how much this appeals to you by the excitement in your voice. I know moving out here wasn't what you wanted."

"No, it was totally what I wanted. I need to be with you. You're my life."

He smiled and stole a tender kiss. "And you're mine, but you've not been really happy here." I had to look away. "I want you to be happy. And this, I think, will make you happy. You'll have animals to take care of and crops to grow."

"Not so sure about the crops," I waved a hand at the scenery.

"Ah, well, okay, maybe not crops but animals. We can have a massive garden! And I'd love some goats. Those little ones."

"And a dog," I sighed. "A red heeler named Rex."

"Yep, a red heeler."

I glanced from the sun creeping into the sky to my husband. "Are you sure you're cool with this idea?"

"I am one thousand percent cool with it."

I tucked a curl behind his ear then brushed his lips with mine. My cell buzzed. I glanced down at the phone resting beside me.

"It's the guy from Legacy Ranch in Texas. Should I take it?"

He nodded and moved close, his hip and thigh pressed to mine. I blew out a deep breath and took the call that would change our lives forever with Ryker at my side. Just as he had always been and would forever be.

EPILOGUE

Ryker

Today's visit to the offices of Lesser, Movvern, and Bligh was very different to the last one. They had a department dealing with property and that was the team we were there to see.

"This place gives me the heebie-jeebies," Colorado groused from where he sat cross-legged on the floor. He'd brought Maddie with him and looked right at home with the colorful wooden blocks and his daughter. "I mean who even has carpet this thick?"

I hadn't even noticed the carpet, but it certainly didn't give me the heebie-jeebies, whatever that felt like. I'd been staring at the landscape of the desert that hung over the reception desk and picturing the house that Jacob had shared a drawing of last night. He'd talked to this guy Jack Campbell-Hayes from Legacy Ranch who'd explained all about *this* and *that* and *whatever*, a lot of it going over my head, because let's face it, horses couldn't skate. Our place would have three bedrooms, a big kitchen, a den, and an office big enough to split in two—one half for hockey, the other for the workings of the as-yet-unnamed ranch. Other rooms and two bathrooms gave us plenty of space to spread out, and construction should be finished on that by September.

The extra parts, the stables, the separate rooms in a block, each with their own bathroom, and a big communal kitchen area, were all on schedule to be done by October. Somehow, by next Christmas the place would be ready to take in people who needed sanctuary from the world outside. Jacob had plans for on-site counselors, and a guy called Steve was coming up from Legacy Ranch to help us work out the kinks. With Jacob taking the check from the university we had a lot of funding covered, but an anonymous deposit of another cool million wasn't going to be sniffed at. I knew it was from Dad and Ten, although we never acknowledged it. Colorado was selling the land to us for a few dollars an acre, much to his accountant's dismay, but he wanted to be part of the ranch, talking about music therapy.

"Mr. Benson, Mr. Madsen, you can come in now." Colorado scooped up Maddie and left with a sketched wave, and then it was just us. We would have loved to hyphenate our names like Dad and Ten, but Benson and Madsen just had no good way of fitting together. Although, Jacob didn't know I'd done this, but the jersey for the new season actually had Benson-Madsen on the back. He'd just smile at me.

He smiled a lot.

What had happened wasn't something we'd forget, but Jacob was a footnote in the mess that was Adam

Isaksson's life. Counseling was still something we did, but it was less frequent now, and the ranch was good medicine for the heart. The signing of the documents was the easy part, everything was in joint names, just the same as the rest of our lives, and all too soon we were back outside the offices and standing in that same alleyway.

This time we kissed and hugged and it was the start of a brand new path for Jacob. And for me.

"Right then," Jacob said, after stealing another heated kiss. "Ready?"

We were leaving soon, heading to England for a delayed honeymoon and attending Seb and Alex's wedding, and we were packed. All we had to do was head back to our apartment, grab the bags, and that was it, two weeks of honeymoon vacation.

"Always ready," I smirked, and got in one more kiss.

"Ry, you know if we keep kissing we'll be here all day." Jacob took my hand and tugged me out of the alley and into the quiet street, but stopped and lifted my hand with the platinum ring, kissed my palm and then closed my fingers into a fist. "Hold that kiss for later."

I made a show of putting it in a pocket, then patted it. "It's always useful to have one spare," I said in all seriousness.

Then, hand in hand we walked away from Lesser, Movvern, and Bligh, and headed straight into the rest of our lives.

THE END

HOCKEY SERIES' FROM RJ SCOTT & V.L. LOCEY

Harrisburg Railers

Owatonna U Hockey

Arizona Raptors

Boston Rebels

LA Storm

Chesterford Coyotes - Young Adult

When hockey wunderkind Tennant Rowe meets his new coach, he knows he's in trouble. Jared Madsen is nine years older than Tennant, impossibly attractive, and — worst of all — his brother's off-limits best friend. Is their chemistry worth the risk?

Changing Lines (Railers 1)

Can Tennant show Jared that age is just a number, and that love is all that matters?

The Rowe Brothers are famous hockey hotshots, but as the youngest of the trio, Tennant has always had to play against his brothers' reputations. To get out of their shadows, and against their advice, he accepts a trade to the Harrisburg Railers, where he runs into Jared Madsen. Mads is an old family friend and his brother's one-time teammate. Mads is Tennant's new coach. And Mads is the sexiest thing he's ever laid eyes on.

Jared Madsen's hockey career was cut short by a fault in his heart, but coaching keeps him close to the game. When Ten is traded to the team, his carefully organized world is thrown into chaos. Nine years his junior and his best friend's brother, he knows Ten is strictly off-limits, but as soon as he sees Ten's moves, on and off the ice, he knows that his heart could get him into trouble again.

Changing Lines

Harrisburg Railers (Hockey Romance)

1. Changing Lines
2. First Season
3. Deep Edge
4. Poke Check
5. Last Defense
6. Goal Line
7. Neutral Zone
8. Hat Trick
9. Save The Date
10. Baby Makes Three
11. Rivals
12. Perfect Gifts
13. Family First

Railers Volume 1 | Railers Volume 2 | Railers Volume 3 | Railers Volume 4

Coast to Coast (Arizona Raptors 1)

Coast To Coast

When opposites attract, this bottom-of-the-league team will never be the same again.

A stipulation in his father's will forces Mark back into the arms of a family that disowned him and leaves him one-third owner of a hockey team facing financial ruin. He doesn't even watch hockey, let alone like it, and wants nothing more than to head back to New York. Then there's the new coach, a stubborn, opinionated, irritating man with superiority issues and questionable music taste. Butting heads with Rowen becomes the new normal, but it comes with passionate debate and an all-consuming lust.

Challenged to rebuild one of the worst teams in the league into a future cup contender, Rowen can't pass up the opportunity. Never in his twenty years of hockey has he ever seen a team managed so badly or coached players overflowing with resentment and bigotry. Yet there's something about this team and this city that compels him to roll up his sleeves and start dismantling. If only Mark, one of three siblings who now own the Raptors, wasn't so damned rock-headed yet so damned appealing his job might be easier. It doesn't look like either is willing to give in, but one night in a dark, desert hotel changes everything.

Coast To Coast

Arizona Raptors (Hockey Romance)

Top Shelf (Boston Rebels 1)

Top Shelf

Acting on the attraction to his best friend's brother has always been off the table for Xander until a passionate hookup with Mason at a beach resort begins a love affair that burns long after summer ends.

Mason specializes in assisting same-sex couples on their journey to becoming parents and fighting every rule that blocks his way in the stuck-in-the-past agency that hired him. Living in his brother's pool house is rent-free, and every cent he earns he saves for his dream—that one day he'd have his own company helping others. The downside is that he has to see his annoying brother every day, the upside is that his brother's teammates from the Boston Rebels make regular visits. The eye candy that passes Mason's window is almost enough to make him consider dating a hockey player, but not just any player though. Ever since Xander—his brother's childhood friend—came out as gay at a press conference, Mason's puppy love has turned into a burning attraction he can no longer ignore.

Hockey has been one of Xander's main focuses since he was old enough to balance on skates. Well, hockey and Mason Kingsley, but Mason was always unattainable. Now that he's about to see thirty candles on his birthday cake and is no longer hiding the fact he's gay, he's ready to find a soul mate to make his life complete. A summer vacation is just what he needs to have time to think, but when the Boston Rebels arriving in paradise with Mason in tow, thinking is the last thing he needs. One torrid night under a balmy moon and rules about not messing with his best friend's brother vanish on a warm, tropical breeze.

Summer romances don't generally last past Labor Day, but with the new season about to begin Xander and Mason are going to have to face the world and decide if their love is real enough to withstand everything.

Top Shelf

Boston Rebels

Lost In Boston (Free Prequel Novella)

1. Top Shelf

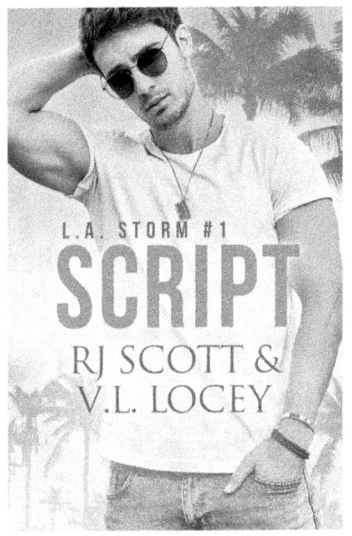

Script (LA Storm, 1)

Script

Hollywood A-lister Finn might be Canadian, but he needs Cameron to show him how to hockey.

Actor Finn Kerrigan is at a crossroads. After growing up a soap star, then starring in a hugely successful trilogy of action movies, he's finally given the chance to read a heartfelt and passionate script that could change his life forever. The role would be enough for people to see him as a serious actor, and maybe even win him an award or two (and no, a golden raspberry award for his action movies doesn't count). Once established as a serious actor he's sure he can come out of the closet and finally live his truth. When he lies to get the part of a hockey player on a struggling team, he suddenly has nowhere to hide. He might be Canadian, but the last time he skated he was ten, and no, he doesn't have hockey in his blood. With only a month until filming starts, he about to be exposed, but partnered with a player who's supposed to be giving him tips, he doesn't realize how many of his secrets will come to light. Falling in lust, one heated kiss at a time, is inevitable, but giving Cameron up at the end of the shoot could break his heart.

Cameron Chavkin is the face of the LA Storm. And the body, and the hair, and the smile. He's at the prime of his career, men and women want to be with him, and he's skating better than he ever has before. His house sits next to a famous rock star's mansion, his garage is filled with expensive cars, and he's even been asked to mentor a once-famous actor in a new hockey movie. Life is pretty sweet. Until the bad boy of hockey meets Finn, a man on the edge with more secrets than Cameron has endorsements. Knowing better than to get involved, Cameron is swept up despite himself, and when it's time to say goodbye to the Storm's most eligible bachelor is finding it hard to follow the script.

Script

LA Storm

Off The Ice (Chesterford Coyotes, 1)

Off The Ice

A coming-of-age love story with high school, hockey rivalry, friendship, family, and coming out.

Soren's life changes in an instant when he and his younger brother are adopted by hockey royalty. Making sense of his new life is hard enough, but when he's enrolled in a private school it means facing a whole new set of problems. Navigating friendship, family, and hockey is one thing, but being attracted to the boy who vexes him is a whole new thing.

Felix has a reputation to protect. He's the kid who seems to have everything but looks can be deceiving. Spinning lies about his perfect life, he's created a fantasy world that even he has started to believe. Only, it's not long before everything crumbles, all of his pretty lies are revealed, and only his closest rival sees through his pain and stands by him.

Fighting is easy, friendship is hard, but love is everything.

Off The Ice

Chesterford Coyotes

1. Off The Ice
2. On Thin Ice
3. *Dance on Ice*

ALSO BY RJ SCOTT

For a full list of ebooks and links please scan the code above or
visit rjscott.co.uk/rjbooks

MEET RJ SCOTT

RJ discovered romance in books at a very young age and realized that if there wasn't romance on the page, she could create it in her head. With over one hundred and fifty books published, she is a full time author of gay romance.

She lives and works out of her home in the beautiful English countryside, spends her spare time reading, watching films, and enjoying time with her family.

The last time she had a week's break from writing she didn't like it one little bit and has yet to meet a box of chocolates she couldn't defeat.

www.rjscott.co.uk | rj@rjscott.co.uk

NEWSLETTER - rjscott.co.uk/rjnews

facebook.com/author.rjscott

x.com/Rjscott_author

instagram.com/rjscott_author

amazon.com/author/rj-scott

bookbub.com/authors/rj-scott

goodreads.com/rjscott

pinterest.com/rjscottauthor

ALSO BY VL LOCEY

For a full list of ebooks and links please scan the code above or
visit vllocey.com/stories-from-vl-locey

MEET V.L. LOCEY

V.L. Locey loves worn jeans, yoga, belly laughs, walking, reading and writing lusty tales, Greek mythology, the New York Rangers, comic books, and coffee.

(Not necessarily in that order.)

She shares her life with her husband, her daughter, one dog, two cats, a flock of assorted domestic fowl, and two Jersey steers.

When not writing spicy romances, she enjoys spending her day with her menagerie in the rolling hills of Pennsylvania with a cup of fresh java in hand.

vllocey.com
vicki@vllocey.com

Newsletter - vllocey.com/newsletter

facebook.com/V.L.Locey
x.com/vllocey
instagram.com/vl_locey
bookbub.com/authors/v-l-locey
goodreads.com/vllocey
pinterest.com/vllocey